Roald Dahl's Heroes and Villains

ROALD DAHL'S HEROES AND VILLAINS
A JONATHAN CAPE BOOK 978 0 857 55125 2
Published in Great Britain by Jonathan Cape,
an imprint of Random House Children's Publishers UK
A Random House Group Company
This edition published 2013

10 9 8 7 6 5 4 3 2 1

THE ENORMOUS CROCODILE first published by Jonathan Cape in 1978
THE GIRAFFE AND THE PELLY AND ME first published by Jonathan Cape in 1985
Edition with new illustrations first published in 1992
THE TWITS first published by Jonathan Cape in 1980
Colour edition published by Puffin Books in 2010
GEORGE'S MARVELLOUS MEDICINE first published by Jonathan Cape in 1981
Colour edition published by Puffin Books in 2011 with colour treatment by Rupert Van Wyk

Set in Bembo

RANDOM HOUSE CHILDREN'S PUBLISHERS UK
61–63 Uxbridge Road, London W5 5SA
www.**randomhousechildrens**.co.uk
www.**randomhouse**.co.uk
Addresses for companies within The Random House Group Limited can be found at:
www.randomhouse.co.uk/offices.htm
THE RANDOM HOUSE GROUP Limited Reg. No. 954009
A CIP catalogue record for this book is available from the British Library.
Printed in China.

The Random House Group Limited supports the Forest Stewardship Council® (FSC®), the leading international forest-certification organisation. Our books carrying the FSC label are printed on FSC®-certified paper. FSC is the only forest-certification scheme supported by the leading environmental organisations, including Greenpeace. Our paper procurement policy can be found at www.randomhouse.co.uk/environment

MIX
Paper from responsible sources
FSC® C104723

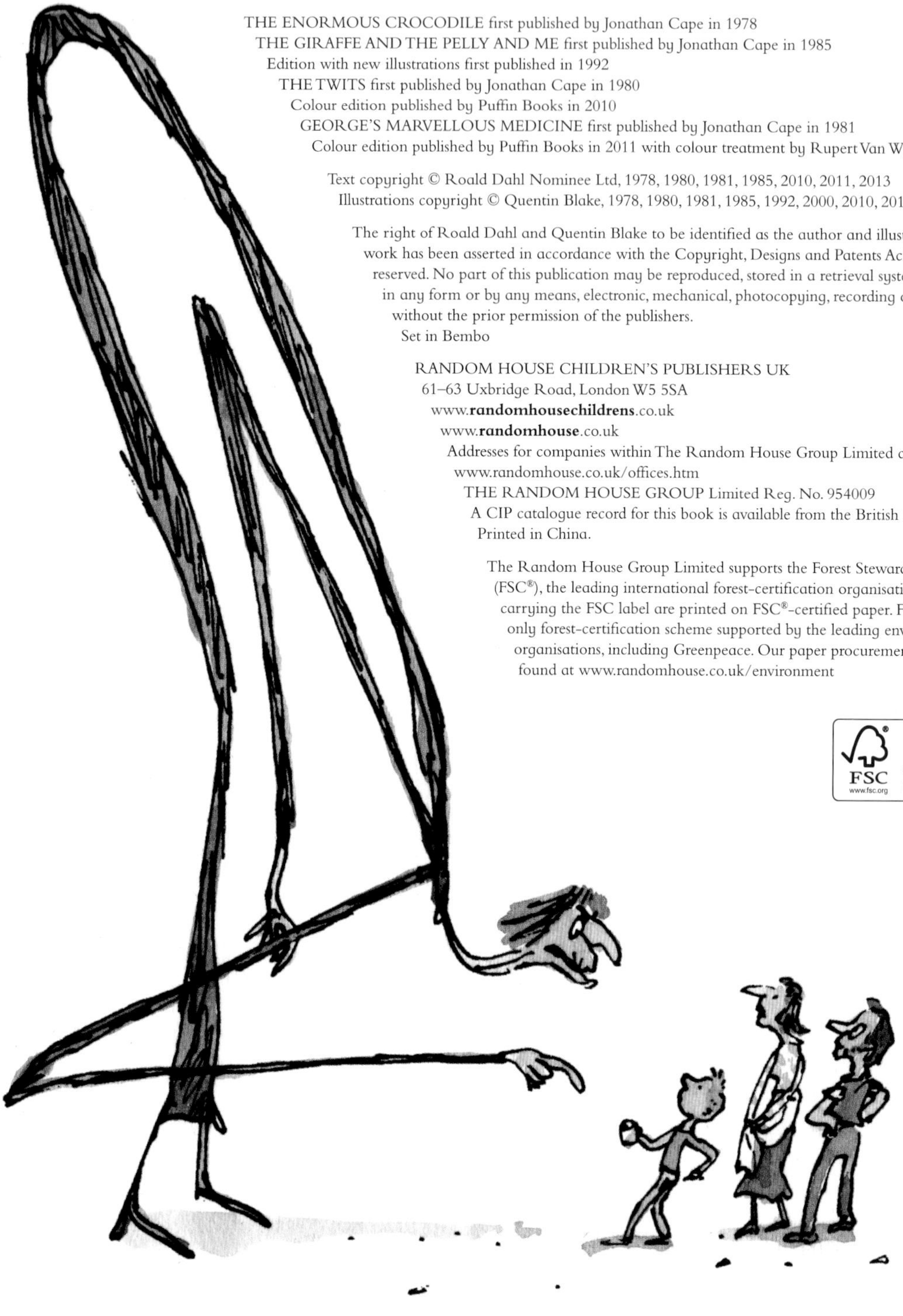

Roald Dahl's Heroes and Villains

illustrated by Quentin Blake

JONATHAN CAPE • LONDON

Contents

THE ENORMOUS CROCODILE 7

THE GIRAFFE
AND THE PELLY AND ME 39

THE TWITS 71

GEORGE'S MARVELLOUS MEDICINE 155

The Enormous Crocodile

To Sophie

R.D.

In the biggest brownest muddiest river in Africa, two crocodiles lay with their heads just above the water. One of the crocodiles was enormous. The other was not so big.

"Do you know what I would like for my lunch today?" the Enormous Crocodile asked.

"No," the Notsobig One said. "What?"

The Enormous Crocodile grinned, showing hundreds of sharp white teeth. "For my lunch today," he said, "I would like a nice juicy little child."

"I never eat children," the Notsobig One said. "Only fish."

"Ho, ho, ho!" cried the Enormous Crocodile. "I'll bet if you saw a fat juicy little child paddling in the water over there at this very moment, you'd gulp him up in one gollop!"

"No, I wouldn't," the Notsobig One said. "Children are too tough and chewy. They are tough and chewy and nasty and bitter."

"*Tough* and *chewy*!" cried the Enormous Crocodile. "*Nasty* and *bitter!* What awful tommy-rot you talk! They are juicy and yummy!"

"They taste so bitter," the Notsobig One said, "you have to cover them with sugar before you can eat them."

"Children are bigger than fish," said the Enormous Crocodile. "You get bigger helpings."

"You are greedy," the Notsobig One said. "You're the greediest croc in the whole river."

"I'm the bravest croc in the whole river," said the Enormous Crocodile. "I'm the only one who dares to leave the water and go through the jungle to the town to look for little children to eat."

"You've only done that once," snorted the Notsobig One. "And what happened then? They all saw you coming and ran away."

"Ah, but today when I go, they won't see me at all," said the Enormous Crocodile.

"Of course they'll see you," the Notsobig One said. "You're so enormous and ugly, they'll see you from miles away."

The Enormous Crocodile grinned again, and his terrible sharp teeth sparkled like knives in the sun. "Nobody will see me," he said, "because this time I've thought up secret plans and clever tricks."

"*Clever tricks?*" cried the Notsobig One. "You've never done anything clever in your life! You're the stupidest croc on the whole river!"

"I'm the cleverest croc on the whole river," the Enormous Crocodile answered. "For my lunch today I shall feast upon a fat juicy little child while you lie here in the river feeling hungry. Goodbye."

The Enormous Crocodile swam to the side of the river, and crawled out of the water.

A gigantic creature was standing in the slimy oozy mud on the river-bank. It was Humpy-Rumpy, the Hippopotamus.

"Hello, hello," said Humpy-Rumpy. "Where on earth are you off to at this time of day?"

"I have secret plans and clever tricks," said the Crocodile.

"Oh dear," said Humpy-Rumpy. "I'll bet you're going to do something horrid."

The Enormous Crocodile grinned at Humpy-Rumpy and said:

"I'm going to fill my hungry empty tummy
With something yummy yummy yummy yummy!"

"What's so yummy?" asked Humpy-Rumpy.

"Try to guess," said the Crocodile. "It's something that walks on two legs."

"You don't mean . . ." said Humpy-Rumpy. "You don't *really* mean you're going to eat a little child?"

"Of course I am," said the Crocodile.

"Oh, you horrid greedy grumptious brute!" cried Humpy-Rumpy. "I hope you get caught and cooked and turned into crocodile soup!"

The Enormous Crocodile laughed out loud at Humpy-Rumpy. Then he waddled off into the jungle.

Inside the jungle, he met Trunky, the Elephant. Trunky was nibbling leaves from the top of a tall tree, and he didn't notice the Crocodile at first. So the Crocodile bit him on the leg.

"Ow!" said Trunky in his big deep voice. "Who did that? Oh, it's you, is it, you beastly Crocodile. Why don't you go back to the big brown muddy river where you belong?"

"I have secret plans and clever tricks," said the Crocodile.

"You mean you've *nasty* plans and *nasty* tricks," said Trunky. "You've never done a nice thing in your life."

The Enormous Crocodile grinned up at Trunky and said:

"I'm off to find a yummy child for lunch.
Keep listening and you'll hear the bones go crunch!"

"Oh, you wicked beastly beast!" cried Trunky. "Oh, you foul and filthy fiend! I hope you get squashed and squished and squizzled and boiled up into crocodile stew!"

The Enormous Crocodile laughed out loud and disappeared into the thick jungle.

A bit further on, he met Muggle-Wump, the Monkey. Muggle-Wump was sitting in a tree, eating nuts.

"Hello, Crocky," said Muggle-Wump. "What are you up to now?"

"I have secret plans and clever tricks," said the Crocodile.

"Would you like some nuts?" asked Muggle-Wump.

"I have better things to eat than nuts," sniffed the Crocodile.

"I didn't think there *was* anything better than nuts," said Muggle-Wump.

"Ah-ha," said the Enormous Crocodile,

"The sort of things that I'm going to eat
Have fingers, toe-nails, arms and legs and feet!"

Muggle-Wump went pale and began to shake all over. "You aren't really going to gobble up a little child, are you?" he said.

"Of course I am," said the Crocodile. "Clothes and all. They taste better with the clothes on."

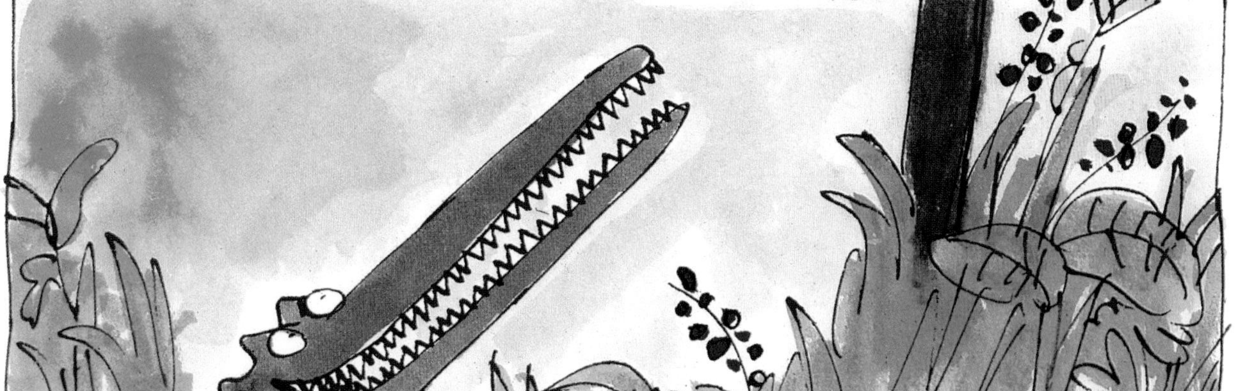

"Oh, you horrid hoggish croc!" cried Muggle-Wump. "You slimy creature! I hope the buttons and buckles all stick in your throat and choke you to death!"

The Crocodile grinned up at Muggle-Wump and said, "I eat monkeys, too." And quick as a flash, with one bite of his huge jaws, he bit through the tree that Muggle-Wump was sitting in, and down it came. But just in time, Muggle-Wump jumped into the next tree and swung away through the branches.

A bit further on, the Enormous Crocodile met the Roly-Poly Bird. The Roly-Poly Bird was building a nest in an orange tree.

"Hello there, Enormous Crocodile!" sang the Roly-Poly Bird. "We don't often see you up here in the jungle."

"Ah," said the Crocodile. "I have secret plans and clever tricks."

"I hope it's not something nasty," sang the Roly-Poly Bird.

"*Nasty!*" cried the Crocodile. "Of course it's not nasty! It's delicious!"

"It's luscious, it's super,
It's mushious, it's duper,
It's better than rotten old fish.
You mash it and munch it,
You chew it and crunch it!
It's lovely to hear it go squish!"

"It must be berries," sang the Roly-Poly Bird. "Berries are my favourite food in the world. Is it raspberries, perhaps? Or could it be strawberries?"

The Enormous Crocodile laughed so much his teeth rattled together like pennies in a moneybox. "Crocodiles don't eat berries," he said. "We eat little boys and girls. And sometimes we eat Roly-Poly Birds, as well." Very quickly, the Crocodile reached up and snapped his jaws at the Roly-Poly Bird. He just missed the Bird, but he managed to catch hold of the long beautiful feathers in its tail. The Roly-Poly Bird gave a shriek of terror and shot straight up into the air, leaving its tail feathers behind in the Enormous Crocodile's mouth.

At last, the Enormous Crocodile came out of the other side of the jungle into the sunshine. He could see the town not far away.

"Ho-ho!" he said, talking aloud to himself. "Ha-ha! That walk through the jungle has made me hungrier than ever. One child isn't going to be nearly enough for me today. I won't be full up until I've eaten at least three juicy little children!"

He started to creep forward towards the town.

The Enormous Crocodile crept over to a place where there were a lot of coconut trees.

He knew that children from the town often came here looking for coconuts. The trees were too tall for them to climb, but there were always some coconuts on the ground that had fallen down.

The Enormous Crocodile quickly collected all the coconuts that were lying on the ground. He also gathered together several fallen branches.

"Now for Clever Trick Number One!" he whispered to himself. "It won't be long before I am eating the first part of my lunch!"

He took all the coconut branches and held them between his teeth. He grasped the coconuts in his front paws. Then he stood straight up in the air, balancing himself on his tail.

He arranged the branches and the coconuts so cleverly that he now looked exactly like a small coconut tree standing among the big coconut trees.

Soon, two children came along. They were brother and sister. The boy was called Toto. His sister was called Mary. They walked around looking for fallen coconuts, but they couldn't find any because the Enormous Crocodile had gathered them all up.

"Oh look!" cried Toto. "That tree over there is much smaller than the others! And it's full of coconuts! I think I could climb that one quite easily if you help me up the first bit."

Toto and Mary ran towards what they thought was the small coconut tree. The Enormous Crocodile peered through the branches, watching them as they came closer and closer. He licked his lips. He began to dribble with excitement.

Suddenly there was a tremendous whooshing noise. It was Humpy-Rumpy, the Hippopotamus. He came crashing and snorting out of the jungle. His head was down low and he was galloping at a terrific speed.

"Look out, Toto!" shouted Humpy-Rumpy. "Look out, Mary! That's not a coconut tree! It's the Enormous Crocodile and he wants to eat you up!"

Humpy-Rumpy charged straight at the Enormous Crocodile. He caught him with his giant head and sent him tumbling and skidding over the ground.

"Ow-eeee!" cried the Crocodile. "Help! Stop! Where am I?"

Toto and Mary ran back to the town as fast as they could.

But crocodiles are tough. It is difficult for even a Hippopotamus to hurt them.

The Enormous Crocodile picked himself up and crept towards the place where the children's playground was.

"Now for Clever Trick Number Two!" he said to himself. "This one is certain to work!"

There were no children in the playground at that moment. They were all in school.

The Enormous Crocodile found a large piece of wood and placed it in the middle of the playground. Then he lay across the piece of wood and tucked in his feet so that he looked almost exactly like a see-saw.

When school was over, the children all came running on to the playground.

"Oh look!" they cried. "We've got a new see-saw!"

They all crowded round, shouting with excitement.

"Bags I have the first go!"

"I'll get on the other end!"

"I want to go first!"

"So do I! So do I!"

Then, a girl who was older than the others said, "It's rather a funny knobbly sort of a see-saw, isn't it? Do you think it'll be safe to sit on?"

"Of course it will!" the others said. "It looks strong as anything!"

The Enormous Crocodile opened one eye just a tiny bit and watched the children who were crowding around him. Soon, he thought, one of them is going to sit on my head, then I will give a jerk and a snap, and after that it will be *yum yum yum*.

At that moment, there was a flash of brown and something jumped into the playground and hopped up on to the top of the swings.

It was Muggle-Wump, the Monkey.

"Run!" Muggle-Wump shouted to the children. "All of you, run, run, run! That's not a see-saw! It's the Enormous Crocodile and he wants to eat you up!"

The children screamed and ran for their lives.

Muggle-Wump disappeared back into the jungle, and the Enormous Crocodile was left all alone in the playground.

He cursed the Monkey and waddled back into the bushes to hide.

"I'm getting hungrier and hungrier!" he said. "I shall have to eat at least four children now before I am full up!"

The Enormous Crocodile crept around the edge of the town, taking great care not to be seen.

He came to a place where they were getting ready to have a fair. There were slides and swings and dodgem-cars and people selling popcorn and candyfloss. There was also a big roundabout.

The roundabout had marvellous wooden creatures for the children to ride on. There were white horses and lions and tigers and mermaids with fishes' tails and fearsome dragons with red tongues sticking out of their mouths.

"Now for Clever Trick Number Three," said the Enormous Crocodile, licking his lips.

When no one was looking, he crept up on to the roundabout and put himself between a wooden lion and a fearsome dragon. He sat up a bit on his back legs and he kept very still. He looked exactly like a wooden crocodile on the roundabout.

Soon, all sorts of children came flocking into the fair. Several of them ran towards the roundabout. They were very excited.

"I'm going to ride on a dragon!" cried one.

"I'm going on a lovely white horse!" cried another.

"I'm going on a lion!" cried the third one.

And one little girl, whose name was Jill, said, "*I'm* going to ride on that funny old wooden crocodile!"

The Enormous Crocodile kept very still, but he could see the little girl coming towards him. "Yummy-yum-yum," he thought. "I'll gulp her up easily in one gollop."

Suddenly there was a *swish* and a *swoosh* and something came swishing and swooshing out of the sky.

It was the Roly-Poly Bird.

He flew round and round the roundabout, singing, "Look out, Jill! Look out! Look out! Don't ride on that crocodile!"

Jill stopped and looked up.

"That's not a wooden crocodile!" sang the Roly-Poly Bird. "It's a real one! It's the Enormous Crocodile from the river and he wants to eat you up!"

Jill turned and ran. So did all the other children. Even the man who was working the roundabout jumped off it and ran away as fast as he could.

The Enormous Crocodile cursed the Roly-Poly Bird and waddled back into the bushes to hide.

"I'm so hungry now," he said to himself, "I could eat six children before I am full up!"

Just outside the town, there was a pretty little field with trees and bushes all round it. This was called The Picnic Place. There were several wooden tables and long benches, and people were allowed to go there and have a picnic at any time.

The Enormous Crocodile crept over to The Picnic Place. There was no one in sight.

"Now for Clever Trick Number Four!" he whispered to himself.

He picked a lovely bunch of flowers and arranged it on one of the tables.

From the same table, he took away one of the benches and hid it in the bushes.

Then he put himself in the place where the bench had been.

By tucking his head under his chest, and by twisting his tail out of sight, he made himself look very much like a long wooden bench with four legs.

Soon, two boys and two girls came along carrying baskets of food. They were all from one family, and their mother had said they could go out and have a picnic together.

"Which table shall we sit at?" said one.

"Let's take the table with the lovely flowers on it," said another.

The Enormous Crocodile kept as quiet as a mouse. "I shall eat them all," he said to himself. "They will come and sit on my back and I will swizzle my head around quickly, and after that it'll be *squish crunch gollop*."

Suddenly a big deep voice from the jungle shouted, "Stand back, children! Stand back! Stand back!"

The children stopped and stared at the place where the voice was coming from.

Then, with a crashing of branches, Trunky the Elephant came rushing out of the jungle.

"That's not a bench you were going to sit on!" he bellowed. "It's the Enormous Crocodile, and he wants to eat you all up!"

Trunky trotted over to the spot where the Enormous Crocodile was standing, and quick as a flash he wrapped his trunk around the Crocodile's tail and hoisted him up into the air.

"Hey! Let me go!" yelled the Enormous Crocodile, who was now dangling upside down. "Let me go! Let me go!"

"No," Trunky said. "I will not let you go. We've all had quite enough of your clever tricks."

Trunky began to swing the Crocodile round and round in the air. At first he swung him slowly.

Then he swung him faster . . .

And FASTER . . .

And FASTER . . .

And FASTER STILL . . .

Soon the Enormous Crocodile was just a blurry circle going round and round Trunky's head.

Suddenly, Trunky let go of the Crocodile's tail, and the Crocodile went shooting high up into the sky like a huge green rocket.
Up and up he went . . .

HIGHER

and

HIGHER . . .

FASTER

and

FASTER . . .

He was going so fast and so high that soon the earth was just a tiny dot miles below.

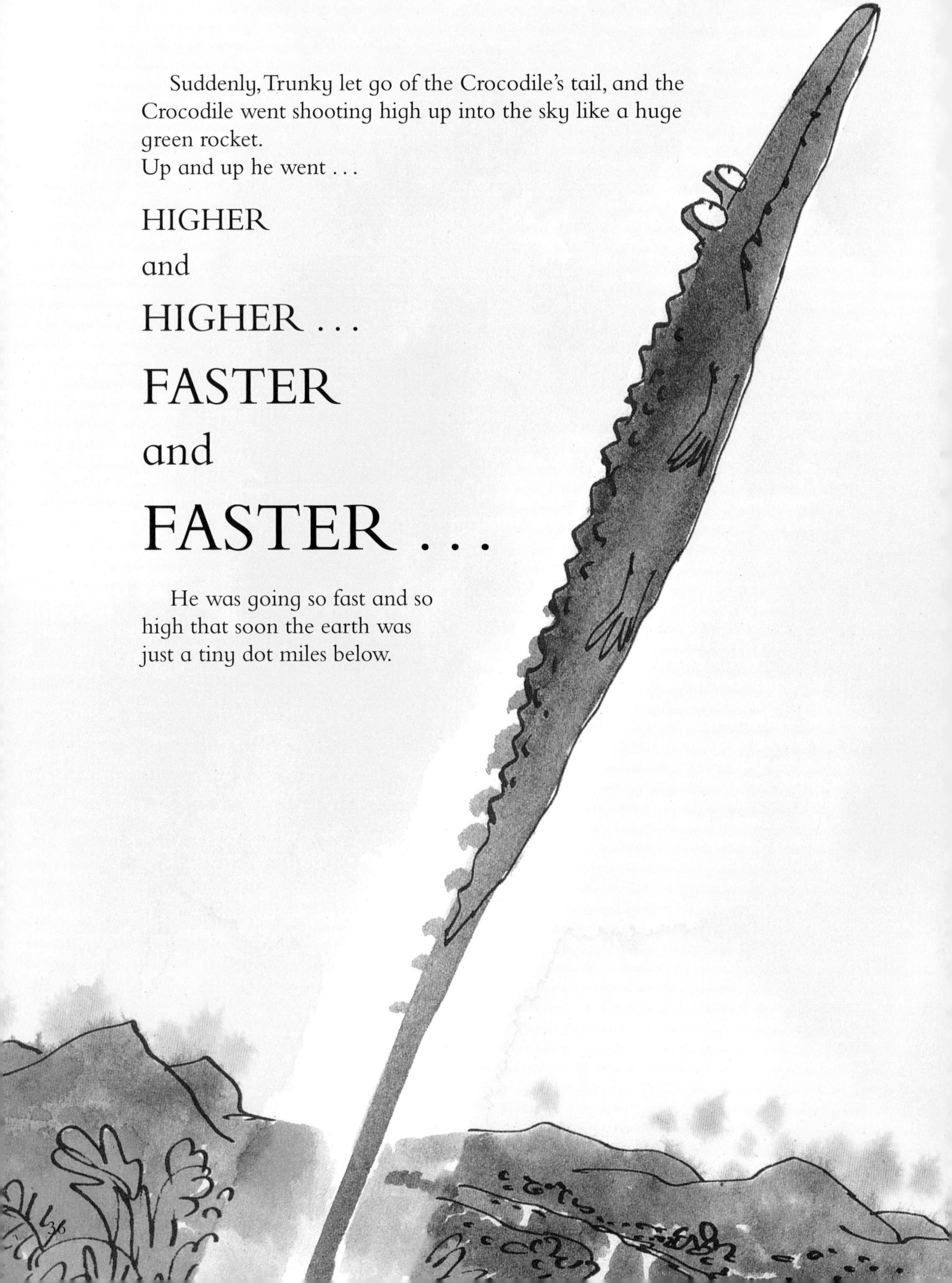

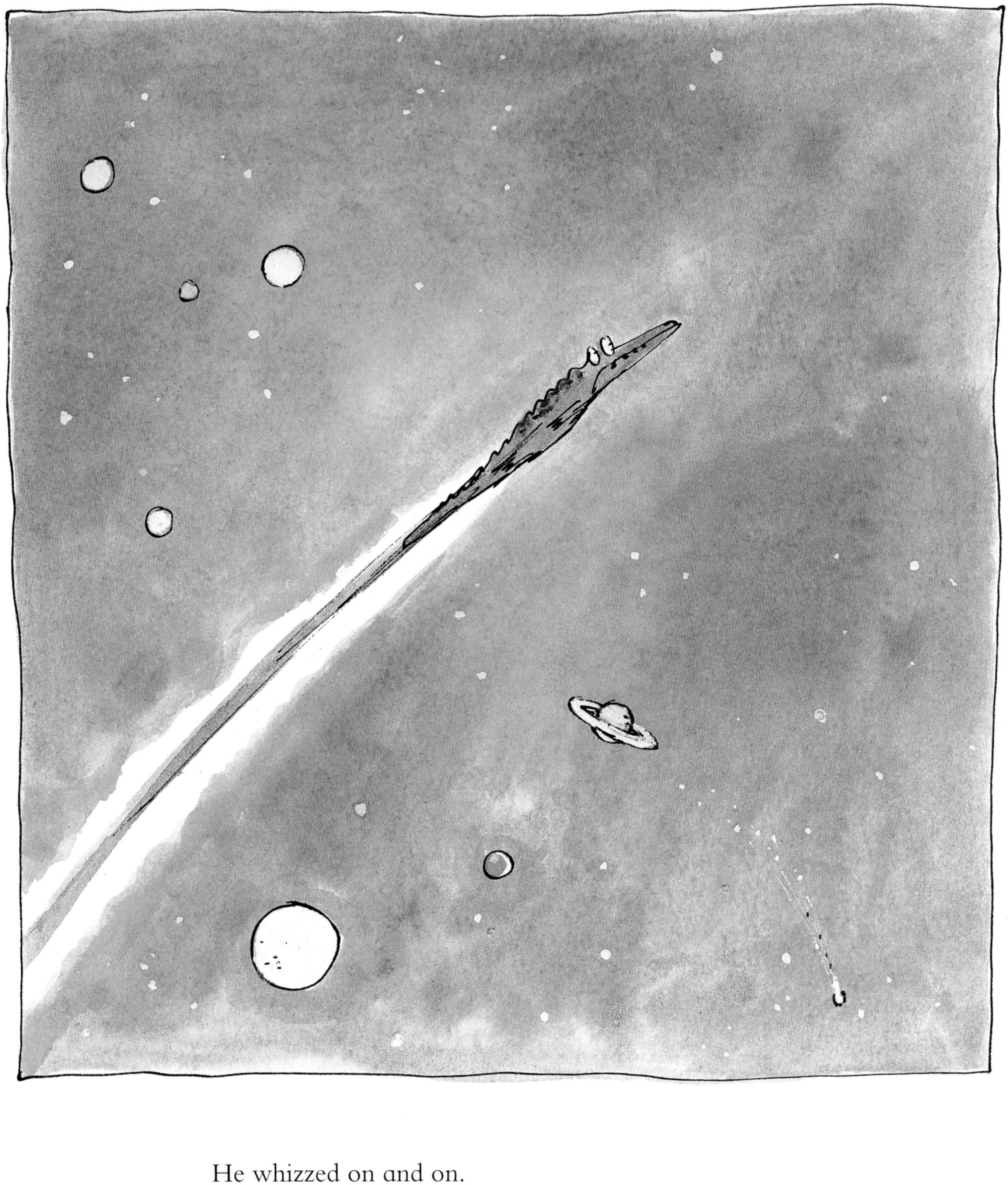

He whizzed on and on.
He whizzed far into space.
He whizzed past the moon.
He whizzed past stars and planets.
Until at last . . .

With the most tremendous

BANG!

the Enormous Crocodile crashed
headfirst into the hot hot sun.

And he was sizzled up like a sausage!

The Giraffe and the Pelly and Me

For
Neisha, Charlotte and Lorina

Not far from where I live there is a queer old empty wooden house standing all by itself on the side of the road. I long to explore inside it but the door is always locked, and when I peer through a window all I can see is darkness and dust. I know the ground floor used once to be a shop because I can still read the faded lettering across the front which says THE GRUBBER. My mother has told me that in our part of the country in the olden days a grubber was another name for a sweet shop, and now every time I look at it I think to myself what a lovely old sweet shop it must have been.

On the shop window itself somebody had painted in white the words FOR SAIL.

One morning, I noticed that FOR SAIL had been scraped off the window and in its place somebody had painted SOLED. I stood there staring at the new writing and wishing like mad that it had been me who had bought it because then I would have been able to make it into a grubber all over again. I have always longed and longed to own a sweet shop. The sweet shop of my dreams would be loaded from top to bottom with Sherbet Suckers and Caramel Fudge and Russian Toffee and Sugar Snorters and Butter Gumballs and thousands and thousands of other glorious things like that. Oh boy, what I couldn't have done with that old Grubber shop if it had been mine!

On my next visit to The Grubber, I was standing across the road gazing at the wonderful old building when suddenly an enormous bathtub came sailing out through one of the second floor windows and crashed right onto the middle of the road!

A few moments later, a white porcelain lavatory pan with the wooden seat still on it came flying out of the same window and landed with a wonderful splintering crash just beside the bathtub. This was followed by a kitchen sink and an empty canary cage and a four-poster bed and two hot-water bottles and a rocking horse and a sewing machine and goodness knows what else besides.

It looked as though some madman was ripping out the whole of the inside of the house, because now pieces of staircase and bits of the banisters and a whole lot of old floorboards came whistling through the windows.

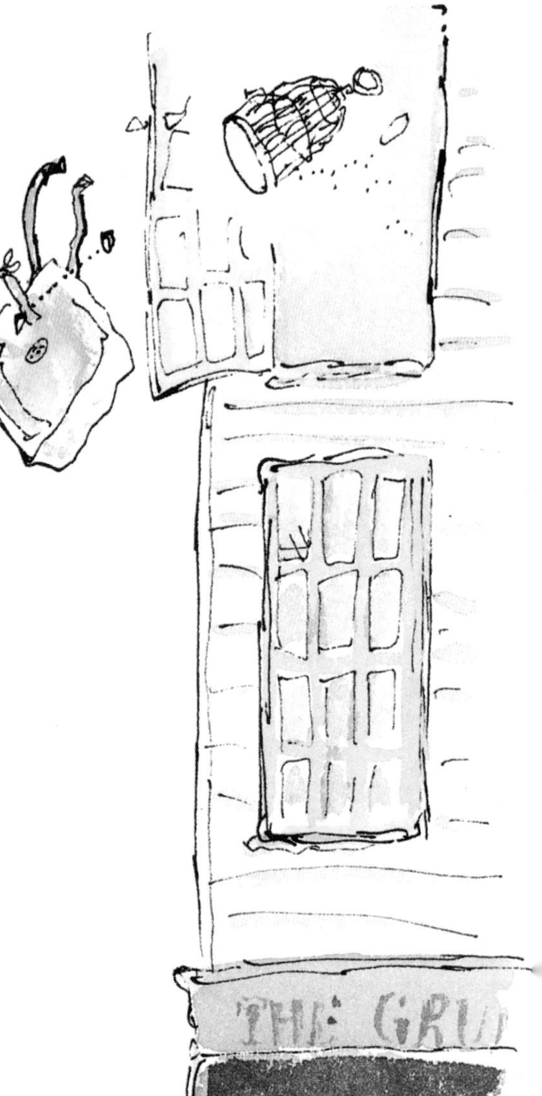

Then there was silence. I waited and waited but not another sound came from within the building. I crossed the road and stood right under the windows and called out, "Is anybody at home?" There was no answer.

In the end it began to get dark so I had to turn away and start walking home. But you can bet your life nothing was going to stop me from hurrying back there again tomorrow morning to see what the next surprise was going to be.

When I got back to the Grubber house the next morning, the first thing I noticed was the new door. The dirty old brown door had been taken out and in its place someone had fitted a brand-new red one. The new door was fantastic. It was twice as high as the other one had been and it looked ridiculous. I couldn't begin to imagine who would want a tremendous tall door like that in his house unless it was a giant.

As well as this, somebody had scraped away the SOLED notice on the shop window and now there was a whole lot of different writing all over the glass. I stood there reading it and reading it and trying to figure out what on earth it all meant.

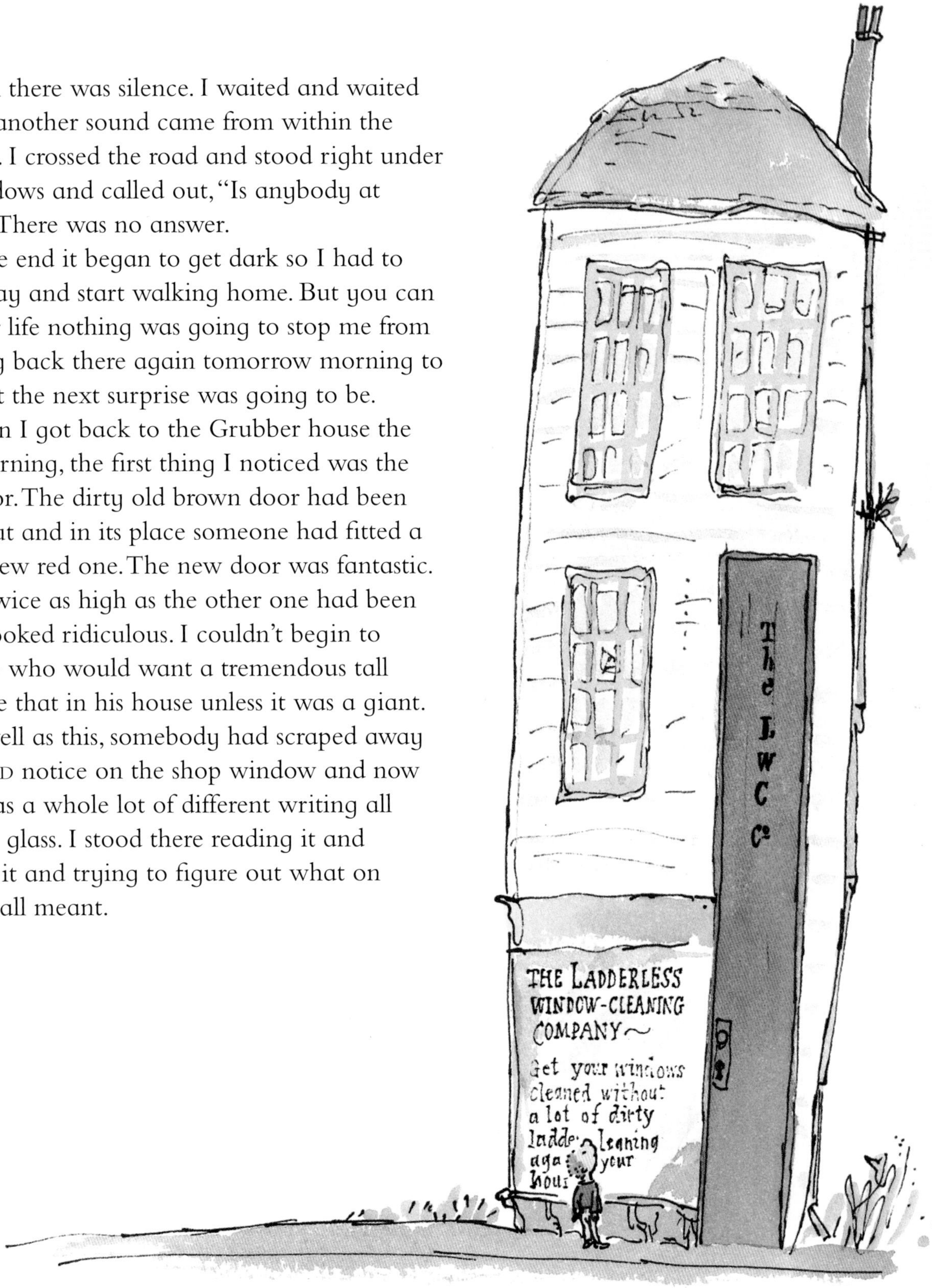

I tried to catch some sign or sound of movement inside the house but there was none . . . until all of a sudden . . . out of the corner of my eye . . . I noticed that one of the windows on the top floor was slowly beginning to open outwards . . .

Then a HEAD appeared at the open window.

I stared at the head. The head stared back at me with big round dark eyes.

Suddenly, a second window was flung wide open and of all the crazy things a gigantic white bird hopped out and perched on the windowsill. I knew what this one was because of its amazing beak, which was shaped like a huge orange-coloured basin. The Pelican looked down at me and sang out:

"Oh, how I wish
For a big fat fish!
I'm as hungry as ever could be!
A dish of fish is my only wish!
How far are we from the sea?"

"We are a long way from the sea," I called back to him, "but there is a fishmonger in the village not far away."

"A fish *what*?"

"A fish*monger*."

"Now what on earth would that be?" asked the Pelican. "I have heard of a fish-*pie* and a fish-*cake* and a fish-*finger*, but I have never heard of a fish-*monger*. Are these mongers good to eat?"

This question baffled me a bit, so I said, "Who is your friend in the next window?"

"She is the Giraffe!" the Pelican answered. "Is she not wonderful? Her legs are on the ground floor and her head is looking out of the top window!"

As if all this wasn't enough, the window on the *first floor* was now flung wide open and out popped a Monkey!

The Monkey stood on the windowsill and did a jiggly little dance. He was so skinny he seemed to be made only out of furry bits of wire, but he danced wonderfully well, and I clapped and cheered and did a little dance myself in return.

"We are the Window-Cleaners!" sang out the Monkey.

"We will polish your glass
Till it's shining like brass
And it sparkles like sun on the sea!
We are quick and polite,
We will come day or night,
The Giraffe and the Pelly and me!

We're a fabulous crew,
We know just what to do,
And we never stop work to drink tea.
All your windows will glow
When we give them a go,
The Giraffe and the Pelly and me!

We use water and soap
Plus some kindness and hope,
But we never use ladders, not we.
Who needs ladders at all
When you're thirty feet tall?
Not Giraffe, and not Pelly! Not me!"

I stood there enthralled. Then I heard the Giraffe saying to the Pelican in the next window, "Pelly, my dear, be so good as to fly down and bring that small person up here to talk to us."

At once the Pelican spread his huge white wings and flew down on to the road beside me. "Hop in," he said, opening his enormous beak.

I stared at the great orange beak and backed away.

"Go on!" the Monkey shouted from up in his window. "The Pelly isn't going to *swallow* you! Climb in!"

I said to the Pelican, "I'll only get in if you promise not to shut your beak once I'm inside."

"You have nothing to fear!" cried the Pelican.

"And let me tell you why.
I have a very special beak!
A special beak have I!
You'll never see a beak so fine,
I don't care where you go.
There's magic in this beak of mine!
Hop in and don't say NO!"

"I will *not* hop in," I said, "unless you swear on your honour you won't shut it once I'm inside. I don't like small dark places."

"When I have done what I am just about to do," said the Pelican, "I won't be *able* to shut it, you don't seem to understand how my beak works."

"Show me," I said.

"Watch this!" cried the Pelican.

I watched in amazement as the top half of the Pelican's beak began to slide smoothly backwards into his head until the whole thing was almost out of sight.

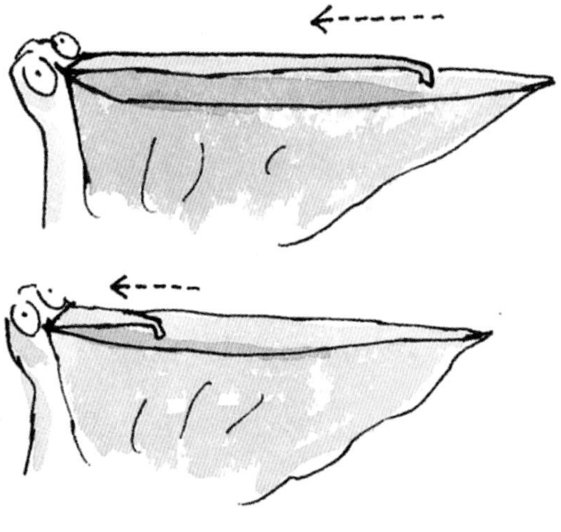

"It bends and goes down inside the back of my neck!" cried the Pelican. "Is that not sensible? Is it not magical?"

"It's unbelievable," I said. "It's exactly like one of those metal tape measures my father's got at home. When it's out, it's straight. When you slide it back in, it bends and disappears."

"Precisely," said the Pelican. "You see, the top half is of no use to me unless I am chewing fish. The bottom half is what counts, my lad! The bottom half of this glorious beak of mine is the bucket in which we carry our window-cleaning water! So if I didn't slide the top half away I'd be standing around all day long holding it open!

"So I slide it away
For the rest of the day!
Even so, I'm still able to speak!
And wherever I've flown
It has always been known
As the Pelican's Patented Beak!

If I want to eat fish
(That's my favourite dish)
All I do is I give it a tweak!
In the blink of an eye
Out it pops! And they cry,
'It's the Pelican's Patented Beak!'"

"Stop showing off down there!" shouted the Monkey from the upstairs window. "Hurry up and bring that small person up to us! The Giraffe is waiting!"

I climbed into the big orange beak, and with a swoosh of wings the Pelican carried me back to his perch on the windowsill.

The Giraffe looked out of her window at me and said, "How do you do? What is your name?"

"Billy," I told her.

"Well, Billy," she said, "we need your help and we need it fast. We *must have* some windows to clean. We've spent every penny we had on buying this house and we've got to earn some more money quickly. The Pelly is starving, the Monkey is famished and I am perishing with hunger. The Pelly needs fish. The Monkey needs nuts and I am even more difficult to feed. I am a Geraneous Giraffe and a Geraneous Giraffe cannot eat anything except the pink and purple flowers of the tinkle-tinkle tree. But those, as I am sure you know, are hard to find and expensive to buy."

The Pelican cried out, "Right now I am so hungry I could eat a stale sardine!

"Has anyone seen a stale sardine
Or a bucket of rotten cod?
I'd eat the lot upon the spot,
I'm such a hungry bod!"

Every time the Pelican spoke, the beak I was standing in jiggled madly up and down, and the more excited he got, the more it jiggled.

The Monkey said, "What Pelly's *really* crazy about is salmon!"

"Yes, yes!" cried the Pelican. "Salmon! Oh, glorious salmon! I dream about it all day long but I never get any!"

"And *I* dream about walnuts!" shouted the Monkey. "A walnut fresh from the tree is scrumptious-galumptious, so flavory-savory, so sweet to eat that it makes me all wobbly just thinking about it!"

At exactly that moment, a huge white Rolls-Royce pulled up right below us, and a chauffeur in a blue and gold uniform got out. He was carrying an envelope in one gloved hand.

"Good heavens!" I whispered. "That's the Duke of Hampshire's car!"

"Who's he?" asked the Giraffe.

"He's the richest man in England!" I said.

The chauffeur knocked on the door of The Grubber.

"We're up here!" the Giraffe called down to him.

He looked up and saw us. He saw the Giraffe, the Pelly, the Monkey and me all staring down at him from above, but not a muscle moved in his face, not an eyebrow was raised. The chauffeurs of very rich men are never surprised by anything they see. The chauffeur said, "His Grace the Duke of Hampshire has instructed me to deliver this envelope to the Ladderless Window-Cleaning Company."

"That's us!" cried the Monkey.

The Giraffe said, "Be so good as to open the envelope and read us the letter."

The chauffeur unfolded the letter and began to read, "'Dear Sirs, I saw your notice as I drove by this morning. I have been looking for a decent window-cleaner for the last fifty years but I have not found one yet. My house has six hundred and seventy-seven windows in it (not counting the greenhouses) and all of them are filthy. Kindly come and see me as soon as possible. Yours truly, Hampshire.' That," added the chauffeur in a voice filled with awe and respect, "was written by His Grace the Duke of Hampshire in his own hand."

The Giraffe said to the chauffeur, "Please tell His Grace the Duke that we will be with him as soon as possible."

The chauffeur touched his cap and got back into the Rolls-Royce.

"Whoopee!" shouted the Monkey.

"Fantastic!" cried the Pelican. "That must be the best window-cleaning job in the world!"

"Billy," said the Giraffe, "what is the house called and how do we get there?"

"It is called Hampshire House," I said. "It's just over the hill. I'll show you the way."

"We're off!" cried the Monkey. "We're off to see the Duke!"

The Giraffe stooped low and went out through the tall door. The Monkey jumped off the windowsill on to the Giraffe's back. The Pelican, with me in his beak hanging on for dear life, flew across and perched on the very top of the Giraffe's head, and away we went.

It wasn't long before we came to the gates of Hampshire House, and as the Giraffe moved slowly up the great wide driveway, we all began to feel just a little bit nervous.

"What's he like, this Duke?" the Giraffe asked me.

"I don't know," I said, "but he's very very famous and very rich. People say he has twenty-five gardeners just to look after his flower-beds."

Soon the huge house itself came into view, and what a house it was! It was like a palace! It was bigger than a palace!

"Just look at those windows!" cried the Monkey. "They'll keep us going for ever!"

Then suddenly we heard a man's voice a short distance away to the right. "I want those big black ones at the top of the tree!" the man was shouting. "Get me those great big black ones!"

We peered round the bushes and saw an oldish man with an immense white moustache standing under a tall cherry tree and pointing his walking stick in the air. There was a ladder against the tree and another man, who was probably a gardener, was up the ladder.

"Get me those great big black juicy ones right at the very top!" the old man was shouting.

"I can't reach them, Your Grace," the gardener called back. "The ladder isn't long enough!"

"Damnation!" shouted the Duke. "I *was* so looking forward to eating those big ones!"

"Here we go!" the Pelican whispered to me, and with a swish and a swoop he carried me up to the very top of the cherry tree and there he perched. "Pick them, Billy!" he whispered. "Pick them quickly and put them in my beak!"

The gardener got such a shock he fell off the ladder. Down below us, the Duke was shouting, "My gun! Get me my gun! Some damnable monster of a bird is stealing my best cherries! Be off with you, sir! Go away! Those are *my* cherries, not yours! I'll have you shot for this, sir! Where *is* my gun?"

"Hurry, Billy!" whispered the Pelican. "Hurry, hurry, hurry!"

"My gun!" the Duke was shouting to the gardener. "Get me my gun, you idiot! I'll have that thieving bird for breakfast, you see if I don't."

"I've picked them all," I whispered to the Pelican.

At once the Pelly flew down and landed right beside the furious figure of the Duke of Hampshire, who was prancing about and waving his stick in the air!

"Your cherries, Your Grace!" I said as I leaned over the edge of the Pelican's beak and offered a handful to the Duke.

The Duke was staggered. He reeled back and his eyes popped nearly out of their sockets. "Great Scott!" he gasped. "Good Lord! What's this? Who are *you*?"

And now the Giraffe, with the Monkey dancing about on her back, emerged suddenly from the bushes. The Duke stared at them. He looked as though he was about to have a fit.

"*Who are these creatures?*" he bellowed. "Has the whole world gone completely dotty?"

"We are the window-cleaners!" sang out the Monkey.

"We will polish your glass
Till it's shining like brass
And it sparkles like sun on the sea!
We will work for Your Grace
Till we're blue in the face,
The Giraffe and the Pelly and me!"

"You *asked* us to come and see you," the Giraffe said.

The truth was at last beginning to dawn on the Duke. He put a cherry into his mouth and chewed it slowly. Then he spat out the stone. "I like the way you picked these cherries for me," he said. "Could you also pick my apples in the autumn?"

"We could! We could! Of course we could!" we all shouted.

"And who are *you*?" the Duke said, pointing his stick at me.

"He is our Business Manager," the Giraffe said. "His name is Billy. We go nowhere without him."

"Very well, very well," the Duke muttered. "Come along with me and let's see if you're any good at cleaning windows."

I climbed out of the Pelican's beak and the kindly old Duke took me by the hand as we all walked towards the house. When we got there, the Duke said, "What happens next?"

"It is all very simple, Your Grace," the Giraffe replied. "I am the ladder, the Pelly is the bucket and the Monkey is the cleaner. Watch us go!"

With that, the famous window-cleaning gang sprang into action. The Monkey jumped down from the Giraffe's back and turned on the garden tap. The Pelican held his great beak under the tap until it was full of water. Then, with a wonderful springy leap the Monkey leaped up once again on to the Giraffe's back. From there he scrambled, as easily as if he were climbing a tree, up the long long neck of the Giraffe until he stood balancing on the very top of her head. The Pelican remained standing on the ground beside us, looking up at the Giraffe.

"We'll do the top floor first!" the Giraffe shouted down. "Bring the water up, please."

The Duke called out, "Don't worry about the two top floors. You can't reach them anyway."

"Who says we can't reach them?" the Giraffe called back.

"I do," the Duke said firmly. "And I'm not having any of you risking your silly necks around here."

If you wish to be friends with a Giraffe, never say anything bad about its neck. Its neck is its proudest possession.

"What's wrong with my neck?" snapped the Giraffe.

"Don't argue with me, you foolish creature!" cried the Duke. "If you can't reach it, you can't reach it and that's the end of it! Now get on with your work!"

"Your Grace," the Giraffe said, giving the Duke a small superior smile, "there are no windows in the world I cannot reach with this magical neck of mine."

The Monkey, who was dancing about most dangerously on top of the Giraffe's head, cried out, "Show him, Giraffey! Go on and show him what you can do with your magical neck!"

The next moment, the Giraffe's neck, which heaven knows was long enough already, began to grow longer . . .
and LONGER . . .
and LONGER . . .
and LONGER . . .

and HIGHER . . .
and HIGHER . . .
and HIGHER . . .

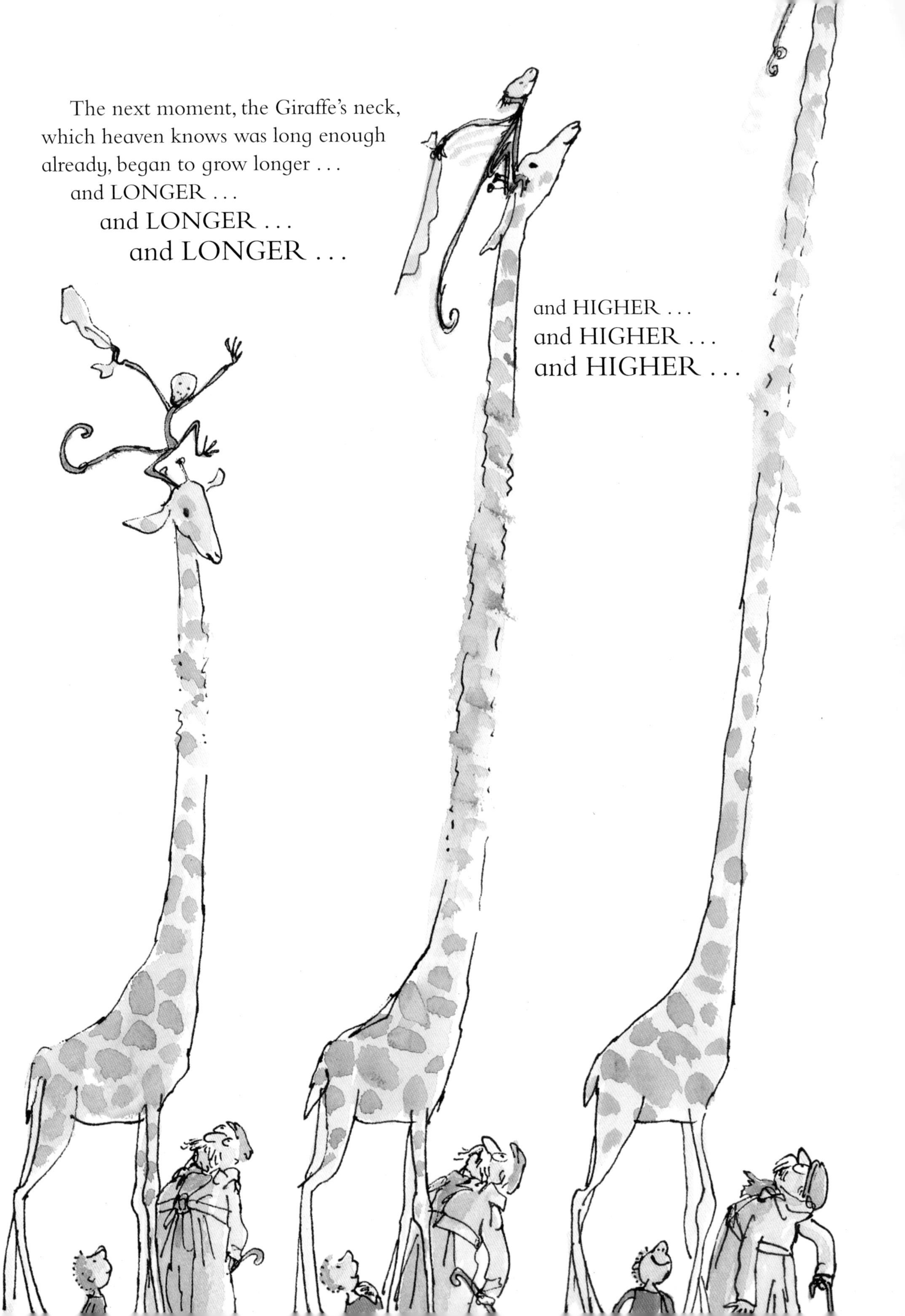

until at last the Giraffe's head with the Monkey on top of it was level with the windows of the top floor.

The Giraffe looked down from her great height and said to the Duke, "How's that?"

The Duke was speechless. So was I. It was the most magical thing I had ever seen, more magical even than the Pelican's Patented Beak.

Up above us, the Giraffe was beginning to sing a little song, but she sang so softly I could hardly catch the words. I think it went something like this:

"My neck can stretch terribly high,
Much higher than eagles can fly.
If I ventured to show
Just how high it would go
You'd lose sight of my head in the sky!"

The Pelican, with his huge beak full of water, flew up and perched on one of the top-floor windowsills near the Monkey, and now the great window-cleaning business really began.

The speed with which the team worked was astonishing. As soon as one window was done, the Giraffe moved the Monkey over to the next one and the Pelican followed. When all the fourth-floor windows on that side of the house were finished, the Giraffe simply drew in her magical neck until the Monkey was level with the third-floor windows and off they went again.

"Amazing!" cried the Duke. "Astonishing! Remarkable! Incredible! I haven't seen out of any of my windows for forty years! Now I shall be able to sit indoors and enjoy the view!"

Suddenly I saw all three of the Window-Cleaners stop dead in their tracks. They seemed to freeze against the wall of the house. None of them moved.

"What's happened to them?" the Duke asked me. "What's gone wrong?"

"I don't know," I answered.

Then the Giraffe, with the Monkey on her head, tiptoed very gingerly away from the house and came towards us. The Pelican flew with them.

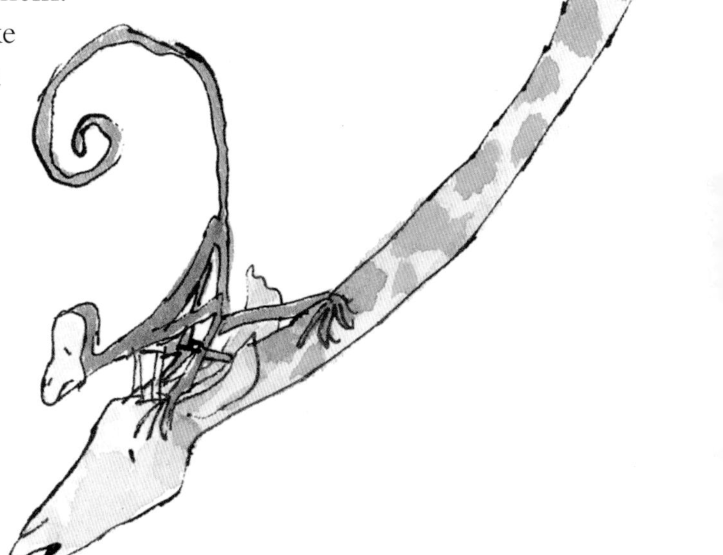

The Giraffe came up very close to the Duke and whispered, "Your Grace, there is a man in one of the bedrooms on the third floor. He is opening all the drawers and taking things out. He's got a pistol!"

The Duke jumped about a foot in the air. "Which room?" he snapped. "Show me at once!"

"It's the one on the third floor where the window is wide open," the Giraffe whispered.

"By Gad!" cried the Duke. "That's the Duchess's bedroom! He's after her jewels! Call the police! Summon the army! Bring up the cannon! Charge with the Light Brigade!" But even as he spoke the Pelican was flying up into the air. As he flew, he turned himself upside down and tipped the window-cleaning water out of his beak. Then I saw the top half of that marvellous patented beak sliding out of his head, ready for action.

"What's that crazy bird up to?" cried the Duke.

"Wait and see," shouted the Monkey. "Hold your breath, old man! Hold your nose! Hold your horses and watch the Pelly go!"

Like a bullet the Pelican flew in through the open window, and five seconds later out he came again with his great orange beak firmly closed. He landed on the lawn beside the Duke.

A tremendous banging noise was coming from inside the Pelican's beak. It sounded as though someone was using a sledge hammer against it from the inside.

"He's got him!" cried the Monkey. "Pelly's got the burglar in his beak!"

"Well done, sir!" shouted the Duke, hopping about with excitement. Suddenly he pulled the handle of his walking stick upwards, and out of the hollow inside of the stick itself he drew a long thin sharp shining sword. "I'll run him through!" he shouted, flourishing the sword like a fencer. "Open up, Pelican! Let me get at him! I'll run the bounder through before he knows what's happened to him! I'll spike him like a pat of butter! I'll feed his gizzards to my foxhounds!"

But the Pelican did not open his beak. He kept it firmly closed and shook his head at the Duke.

The Giraffe shouted, "The burglar is armed with a pistol, Your Grace! If Pelly lets him out now he'll shoot us all."

"He can be armed with a *machine-gun* for all I care!" bellowed the Duke, his massive moustaches bristling like brushwood. "I'll handle the blighter! Open up, sir! Open up!"

Suddenly there was an ear-splitting BANG and the Pelican leaped twenty feet into the air. So did the Duke.

"Watch out!" the Duke shouted, taking ten rapid paces backwards. "He's trying to shoot his way out!" And pointing his sword at the Pelican, he bellowed, "Keep that beak closed, sir! Don't you dare let him out! He'll murder us all!"

"Shake him up, Pelly!" cried the Giraffe. "Rattle his bones! Teach him not to do it again!"

The Pelican shook his head so fast from side to side that the beak became a blur and the man inside must have felt he was being scrambled like eggs.

"Well done, Pelly!" cried the Giraffe. "You're doing a great job! Keep on shaking him so he doesn't fire that pistol again!"

At this point, a lady with an enormous chest and flaming orange hair came flying out of the house screaming, "My jewels! Somebody's stolen my jewels! My diamond tiara! My diamond necklace! My diamond bracelets! My diamond earrings! My diamond rings! They've had the lot! My rooms have been ransacked!" And then this massive female, who fifty-five years ago had been a world-famous opera singer, suddenly burst into song.

"My diamonds are over the ocean,
My diamonds are over the sea,
My diamonds were pinched from my bedroom,
Oh, bring back my diamonds to me."

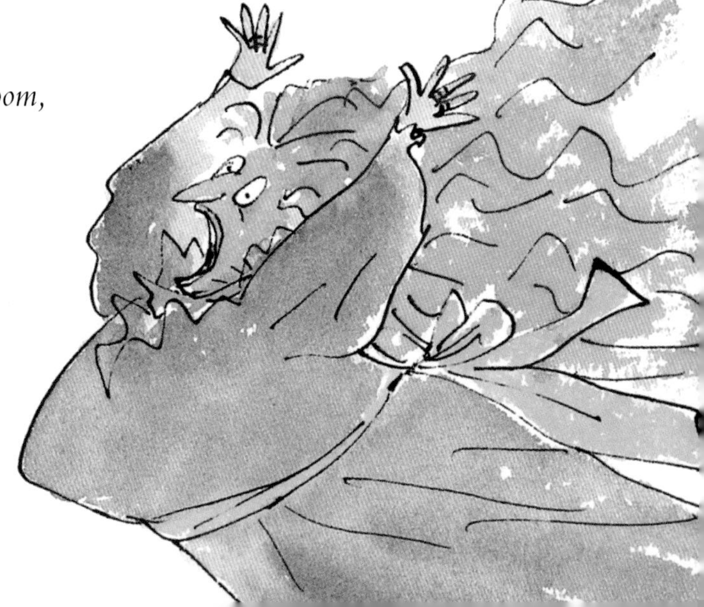

We were so bowled over by the power of the lady's lungs that all of us, excepting the Pelican, who had to keep his beak closed, joined in the chorus.

"Bring back, bring back,
Oh bring back my diamonds to me, to me.
Bring back, bring back,
Oh, bring back my diamonds to me!"

"Calm yourself, Henrietta," said the Duke. He pointed to the Pelican and said, "This clever bird, this brilliant burglar-catching creature has saved the day! The bounder's in his beak!"

The Duchess stared at the Pelican. The Pelican stared back at the Duchess and gave her a wink.

"If he's in there," cried the Duchess, "why don't you let him out! Then you can run him through with that famous sword of yours! I want my diamonds! Open your beak, bird!"

"No, no!" shouted the Duke. "He's got a pistol! He'll murder us all!"

Someone must have called the police because suddenly no less than four squad cars came racing towards us with their sirens screaming.

Within seconds we were surrounded by six policemen, and the Duke was shouting to them, "The villain you are after is inside the beak of that bird! Stand by to collar him!" And to the Pelican he said, "Get ready to open up! Are you ready . . . steady . . . *go*! Open her up!"

The Pelican opened his gigantic beak and immediately the policemen pounced upon the burglar who was crouching inside. They snatched his pistol away from him and dragged him out and put handcuffs on his wrists.

"Great Scott!" shouted the Chief of Police. "It's the Cobra himself!"

"The who! The what!" everyone asked. "Who's the Cobra?"

"The Cobra is the cleverest and most dangerous cat burglar in the world!" said the Chief of Police. "He must have climbed up the drainpipe. The Cobra can climb up anything!"

"My diamonds!" screamed the Duchess. "I want my diamonds! Where are my diamonds?"

"Here they are!" cried the Chief of Police, fishing great handfuls of jewellery from the burglar's pockets.

The Duchess was so overcome with relief that she fell to the ground in a faint.

When the police had taken away the fearsome burglar known as the Cobra, and the fainting Duchess had been carried into the house by her servants, the old Duke stood on the lawn with the Giraffe, the Pelican, the Monkey and me.

"Look!" cried the Monkey. "That rotten burglar's bullet has made a hole in poor Pelly's beak!"

"That's done it," said the Pelican. "Now it won't be any use for holding water when we clean the windows."

"Don't you worry about that, my dear Pelly," said the Duke, patting him on the beak. "My chauffeur will soon put a patch over it the same way he mends the tyres on the Rolls. Right now we have far more important things to talk about than a little hole in a beak."

We stood there waiting to see what the Duke was going to say next.

"Now listen to me, all of you," he said. "Those diamonds were worth millions! Millions and millions! And *you* have saved them!" The Monkey nodded. The Giraffe smiled. The Pelican blushed.

"No reward is too great for you," the Duke went on. "I am therefore going to make you an offer which I hope will give you pleasure. I hereby invite the Giraffe and the Pelican and the Monkey to live on my estate for the rest of their lives.

"I shall give you my best and largest hay barn as your private house. Central heating, showers, a kitchen and anything else you desire for your comfort will be installed.

"In return, you will keep my windows clean, and pick my cherries and my apples. If the Pelican is willing, perhaps he will also give me a ride in his beak now and again."

"A pleasure, Your Grace!" cried the Pelican. "Would you like a ride now?"

"Later," said the Duke. "I'll have one after tea."

At this point, the Giraffe gave a nervous little cough and looked up at the sky.

"Is there a problem?" asked the Duke. "If there is, do please let me hear it."

"I don't like to sound ungrateful or pushy," murmured the Giraffe, "but we do have one very pressing problem. We are all absolutely famished. We haven't eaten for days."

"My *dear* Giraffey!" cried the Duke. "How very thoughtless of me. Food is no problem around here."

"I'm afraid it is not quite as easy as all that," said the Giraffe. "You see, I myself happen to be . . ."

"Don't tell me!" cried the Duke. "I know it already! I am an expert on the animals of Africa. The moment I saw you I knew you were no ordinary giraffe. You are of the Geraneous variety, are you not?"

"You are absolutely right, Your Grace," said the Giraffe. "But the trouble with us is that we only eat . . ."

"You don't have to tell me that either!" cried the Duke. "I know perfectly well a Geraneous Giraffe can eat only one kind of food. Am I not right in thinking that the pink and purple flowers of the tinkle-tinkle tree are your only diet?"

"Yes," sighed the Giraffe, "and that's been my problem ever since I arrived on these shores."

"That is no problem at all here at Hampshire House," said the Duke. "Look over there, my dear Giraffey, and you will see the only plantation of tinkle-tinkle trees in the entire country!"

The Giraffe looked. She gave a gasp of astonishment, and at first she was so overwhelmed she couldn't even speak. Great tears of joy began running down her cheeks.

"Help yourself," said the Duke. "Eat all you want."

"Oh, my sainted souls!" gasped the Giraffe. "Oh, my naked neck! I cannot *believe* what I am seeing!"

The next moment she was galloping full speed across the lawns and whinnying with excitement and the last we saw of her, she was burying her head in the beautiful pink and purple flowers that blossomed on the tops of the trees all around her.

"As for the Monkey," the Duke went on, "I think he also will be pleased with what I have to offer. All over my estate there are thousands of giant nut trees . . ."

"Nuts?" cried the Monkey. "What kind of nuts?"

"Walnuts, of course," said the Duke.

"***Walnuts!***" screamed the Monkey. "Not *walnuts*? You don't really mean *walnuts*? You're pulling my leg! You're joking! You can't be serious! I must have heard wrong!"

"There's a walnut tree right over there," the Duke said, pointing.

The Monkey took off like an arrow, and a few seconds later he was high up in the branches of the walnut tree, cracking the nuts and guzzling what was inside.

"That leaves only the Pelly," said the Duke.

"Yes," said the Pelican nervously, "but I'm afraid that what I eat does not grow on trees. I only eat fish. Would it be too much trouble, I wonder, if I were to ask you for a reasonably fresh piece of haddock or cod every day?"

"Haddock or cod!" shouted the Duke, spitting out the words as though they made a bad taste in his mouth. "Cast your eyes, my dear Pelly, over there to the south."

The Pelican looked across the vast rolling estate and in the distance he saw a great river.

"That is the River Hamp!" cried the Duke. "The finest salmon river in the whole of Europe!"

"***Salmon!***" screeched the Pelican. "Not *salmon*? You don't really mean *salmon*?"

"It's *full* of salmon," the Duke said, "and I own it. You can help yourself."

Before he had finished speaking the Pelican was in the air. The Duke and I watched him as he flew full speed towards the river. We saw him circle over the water, then he dived and disappeared. A few moments later, he was in the air again, and he had a gigantic salmon in his beak.

I stood alone with the Duke on the lawn beside his great house. "Well, Billy," he said, "I'm glad they are all happy. But what about you, my lad? I am wondering if you happen to have just one extra special little wish all for yourself. If you do, I'd love you to tell me about it."

There was a sudden tingling in my toes. It felt as though something tremendous might be going to happen to me any moment.

"Yes," I murmured nervously, "I do have one extra special little wish."

"And what might that be?" said the Duke in a kindly voice.

"There is an old wooden house near where I live," I said. "It's called The Grubber and long ago it used to be a sweet shop. I have wished and wished that one day somebody might come along and make it into a marvellous new sweet shop all over again."

"Somebody?" cried the Duke. "What do you mean, *somebody?* You and I will do that! We'll do it together! We'll make it into the most wonderful sweet shop in the world! And *you*, my boy, will own it!"

Whenever the old Duke got excited, his enormous moustaches started to bristle and jump about. Right now they were jumping up and down so much it looked as though he had a squirrel on his face. "By Gad, sir!" he cried, waving his stick. "I shall buy the place today! Then we'll all get to work and have the whole thing ready in no time! You just wait and see what sort of a sweet shop we are going to make out of this Grubber place of yours!"

It was amazing how quickly things began to happen after that. There was no problem about buying the house because it was owned by the Giraffe and the Pelly and the Monkey, and they insisted upon giving it to the Duke for nothing.

Then builders and carpenters moved in and rebuilt the whole of the inside so that once again it had three floors. On all these floors they put together rows and rows of tall shelves, and there were ladders to climb up to the highest shelves and baskets to carry what you bought.

Then the sweets and chocs and toffees and fudges and nougats began pouring in to fill the shelves. They came by aeroplane from every country in the world, the most wild and wondrous things you could ever imagine.

There were Gumtwizzlers and Fizzwinkles from China, Frothblowers and Spitsizzlers from Africa, Tummyticklers and Gobwangles from the Fiji Islands and Liplickers and Plushnuggets from the Land of the Midnight Sun.

For two whole weeks the flood of boxes and sacks continued to arrive. I could no longer keep track of all the countries they came from, but you can bet your life that as I unpacked each new batch I sampled it carefully. I can remember especially the Giant Wangdoodles from Australia, every one with a huge ripe red strawberry hidden inside its crispy chocolate crust . . . and the Electric Fizzcocklers that made every hair on your head stand straight up on end as soon as you popped one into your mouth . . . and there were Nishnobblers and Gumglotters and Blue Bubblers and Sherbet Slurpers and Tongue Rakers, and as well as all this, there was a whole lot of splendid stuff from the great Wonka factory itself, for example the famous Willy Wonka Rainbow Drops – suck them and you can spit in seven different colours. And his Stickjaw for talkative parents. And his Mint Jujubes that will give the boy next door green teeth for a month.

On the Grand Opening Day, I decided to allow all my customers to help themselves for free, and the place was so crowded with children you could hardly move. The television cameras and the newspaper reporters were all there, and the old Duke himself stood outside in the road with my friends the Giraffe and the Pelly and the Monkey watching the marvellous scene. I came out of the shop to join them for a few moments and I brought each of them a bag of extra special sweets as a present.

To the Duke, because the weather was a little chilly, I gave some Scarlet Scorchdroppers that had been sent to me from Iceland. The label said that they were guaranteed to make the person who sucked them as warm as toast even if he were standing stark naked at the North Pole in midwinter. The moment the Duke popped one into his mouth, thick smoke came gushing out of the old boy's nostrils in such quantities that I thought his moustaches were going up in flames. "Terrific!" he cried, hopping about. "Tremendous stuff! I'll take a case of them home with me!"

To the Giraffe I gave a bag of Glumptious Globgobblers. The Globgobbler is an especially delicious sweet that is made somewhere near Mecca, and the moment you bite into it, all the perfumed juices of Arabia go squirting down your gullet one after the other. "It's wonderful!" cried the Giraffe as a cascade of lovely liquid flavours poured all the way down her long long throat. "It's even better than my favourite pink and purple flowers!"

To the Pelican I gave a big bag of Pishlets. Pishlets, as you probably know, are bought by children who are unable to whistle a tune as they walk along the street but long to do so. They had a splendid effect upon the Pelican, for after he had put one of them into his beak and chewed it for a while, he suddenly started singing like a nightingale. This made him wildly excited because Pelicans are not songbirds. No Pelican had ever been known to whistle a tune before.

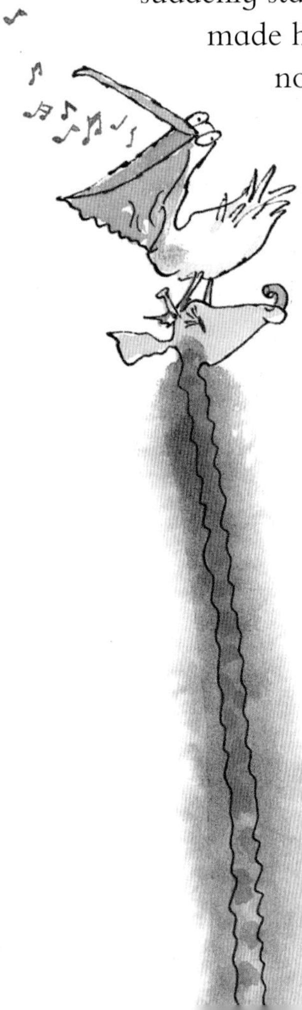

To the Monkey I gave a bag of Devil's Drenchers, those small fiery black sweets that one is not allowed to sell to children under four years old. When you have sucked a Devil's Drencher for a minute or so, you can set your breath alight and blow a huge column of fire twenty feet into the air. The Duke put a match to the Monkey's breath and shouted, "Blow, Monkey, blow!" A sheet of orange flame shot up as high as the roof of the Grubber house and it was wonderful.

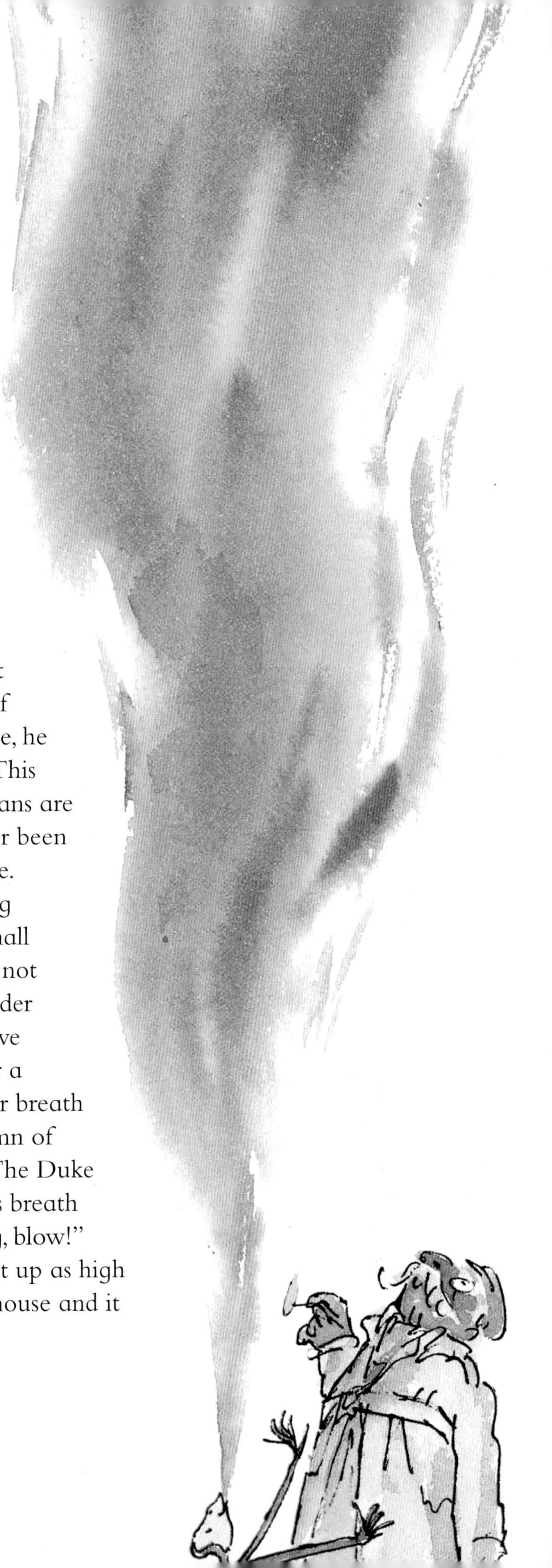

"I've got to leave you now," I said. "I must go and look after my customers in the shop."

"We must go, too," said the Giraffe. "We have one hundred windows to clean before dark."

I said goodbye to the Duke, and then one by one I said goodbye to the three best friends I had ever had. Suddenly, we all became very quiet and melancholy, and the Monkey looked as though he was about to cry as he sang me a little song of farewell:

"We have tears in our eyes
As we wave our goodbyes,
We so loved being with you, we three.
So do please now and then
Come and see us again,
The Giraffe and the Pelly and me.

All you do is to look
At a page in this book
Because that's where we always will be.
No book ever ends
When it's full of your friends
The Giraffe and the Pelly and me."

The Twits

~ For Emma ~

Chapter One

HAIRY FACES

What a lot of hairy-faced men there are around nowadays.

When a man grows hair all over his face it is impossible to tell what he really looks like.

Perhaps that's why he does it. He'd rather you didn't know.

Then there's the problem of washing.

When the very hairy ones wash their faces, it must be as big a job as when you and I wash the hair on our heads.

So what I want to know is this. How often do all these hairy-faced men wash their faces? Is it only once a week, like us, on Sunday nights? And do they shampoo it? Do they use a hairdryer? Do they rub hair-tonic in to stop their faces from going bald? Do they go to a barber to have their hairy faces cut and trimmed or do they do it themselves in front of the bathroom mirror with nail-scissors?

I don't know. But next time you see a man with a hairy face (which will probably be as soon as you step out on to the street) maybe you will look at him more closely and start wondering about some of these things.

Chapter Two

MR TWIT

Mr Twit was one of these very hairy-faced men. The whole of his face except for his forehead, his eyes and his nose was covered with thick hair. The stuff even sprouted in revolting tufts out of his nostrils and ear-holes.

Mr Twit felt that this hairiness made him look terrifically wise and grand. But in truth he was neither of these things. Mr Twit was a twit. He was born a twit. And now at the age of sixty, he was a bigger twit than ever.

The hair on Mr Twit's face didn't grow smooth and matted as it does on most hairy-faced men. It grew in spikes that stuck out straight like the bristles of a nailbrush.

And how often did Mr Twit wash this bristly nailbrushy face of his?

The answer is NEVER, not even on Sundays.

He hadn't washed it for years.

Chapter Three

Dirty Beards

As you know, an ordinary unhairy face like yours or mine simply gets a bit smudgy if it is not washed often enough, and there's nothing so awful about that.

But a hairy face is a very different matter. Things *cling* to hairs, especially food. Things like gravy go right in among the hairs and stay there. You and I can wipe our smooth faces with a flannel and we quickly look more or less all right again, but the hairy man cannot do that.

We can also, if we are careful, eat our meals without spreading food all over our faces. But not so the hairy man. Watch carefully next time you see a hairy man eating his lunch and you will notice that even if he opens his mouth very wide, it is impossible for him to get a spoonful of beef-stew or ice-cream and chocolate sauce into it without leaving some of it on the hairs.

Mr Twit didn't even bother to open his mouth wide when he ate. As a result (and because he never washed) there were always hundreds of bits of old breakfasts and lunches and suppers sticking to the hairs around his face. They weren't big bits, mind you, because he used to wipe those off with the back of his hand or on his sleeve while he was eating. But if you looked closely (not that you'd ever want to) you would see tiny little specks of dried-up scrambled eggs stuck to the hairs, and spinach and tomato ketchup and fish fingers and minced chicken livers and all the other disgusting things Mr Twit liked to eat.

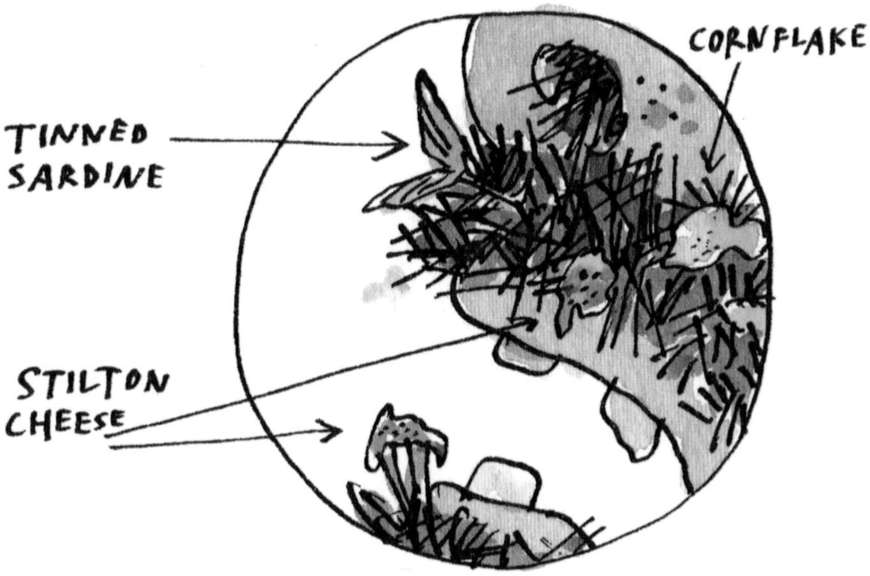

If you looked closer still (hold your noses, ladies and gentlemen), if you peered deep into the moustachy bristles sticking out over his upper lip, you would probably see much larger objects that had escaped the wipe of his hand, things that had been there for months and months, like a piece of maggoty green cheese or a mouldy old cornflake or even the slimy tail of a tinned sardine.

Because of all this, Mr Twit never went really hungry. By sticking out his tongue and curling it sideways to explore the hairy jungle around his mouth, he was always able to find a tasty morsel here and there to nibble on.

What I am trying to tell you is that Mr Twit was a foul and smelly old man.

He was also an extremely horrid old man, as you will find out in a moment.

Chapter Four

Mrs Twit

Mrs Twit was no better than her husband.

She did not, of course, have a hairy face. It was a pity she didn't because that at any rate would have hidden some of her fearful ugliness.

Take a look at her.

Have you ever seen a woman with an uglier face than that? I doubt it.

But the funny thing is that Mrs Twit wasn't born ugly. She'd had quite a nice face when she was young. The ugliness had grown upon her year by year as she got older.

Why would that happen?

I'll tell you why.

If a person has ugly thoughts, it begins to show on the face. And when that person has ugly thoughts

every day,
every week,
every year,

the face gets uglier and uglier until it gets so ugly you can hardly bear to look at it.

A person who has good thoughts cannot ever be ugly. You can have a wonky nose and a crooked mouth and a double chin and stick-out teeth, but if you have good thoughts they will shine out of your face like sunbeams and you will always look lovely.

Nothing shone out of Mrs Twit's face.

In her right hand she carried a walking-stick. She used to tell people that this was because she had warts growing on the sole of her left foot and walking was painful. But the real reason she carried a stick was so that she could hit things with it, things like dogs and cats and small children.

And then there was the glass eye. Mrs Twit had a glass eye that was always looking the other way.

Chapter Five

The Glass Eye

You can play a lot of tricks with a glass eye because you can take it out and pop it back in again any time you like. You can bet your life Mrs Twit knew all the tricks.

One morning she took out her glass eye and dropped it into Mr Twit's mug of beer when he wasn't looking.

Mr Twit sat there drinking the beer slowly. The froth made a white ring on the hairs around his mouth. He wiped the white froth on to his sleeve and wiped his sleeve on his trousers.

'You're plotting something,' Mrs Twit said, keeping her back turned so he wouldn't see that she had taken out her glass eye. 'Whenever you go all quiet like that I know very well you're plotting something.'

Mrs Twit was right. Mr Twit was plotting away like mad. He was trying to think up a really nasty trick he could play on his wife that day.

'You'd better be careful,' Mrs Twit said, 'because when I see you starting to plot, I watch you like a wombat.'

'Oh, do shut up, you old hag,' Mr Twit said. He went on drinking his beer, and his evil mind kept working away on the latest horrid trick he was going to play on the old woman.

Suddenly, as Mr Twit tipped the last drop of beer down his throat, he caught sight of Mrs Twit's awful glass eye staring up at him from the bottom of the mug. It made him jump.

'I told you I was watching you,' cackled Mrs Twit. 'I've got eyes everywhere so you'd better be careful.'

Chapter Six

The Frog

To pay her back for the glass eye in his beer, Mr Twit decided he would put a frog in Mrs Twit's bed.

He caught a big one down by the pond and carried it back secretly in a box.

That night, when Mrs Twit was in the bathroom getting ready for bed, Mr Twit slipped the frog between her sheets. Then he got into his own bed and waited for the fun to begin.

Mrs Twit came back and climbed into her bed and put out the light. She lay there in the dark scratching her tummy. Her tummy was itching. Dirty old hags like her always have itchy tummies.

Then all at once she felt something cold and slimy crawling over her feet. She screamed.

'What's the matter with you?' Mr Twit said.

'Help!' screamed Mrs Twit, bouncing about. 'There's something in my bed!'

'I'll bet it's that Giant Skillywiggler I saw on the floor just now,' Mr Twit said.

'That *what*?' screamed Mrs Twit.

'I tried to kill it but it got away,' Mr Twit said. 'It's got teeth like screwdrivers!'

'Help!' screamed Mrs Twit. 'Save me! It's all over my feet!'

'It'll bite off your toes,' said Mr Twit.

Mrs Twit fainted.

Mr Twit got out of bed and fetched a jug of cold water. He poured the water over Mrs Twit's head to revive her. The frog crawled up from under the sheets to get near the water. It started jumping about on the pillow. Frogs love water. This one was having a good time.

When Mrs Twit came to, the frog had just jumped on to her face. This is not a nice thing to happen to anyone in bed at night. She screamed again.

'By golly it *is* a Giant Skillywiggler!' Mr Twit said. 'It'll bite off your nose.'

Mrs Twit leapt out of bed and flew downstairs and spent the night on the sofa. The frog went to sleep on her pillow.

Chapter Seven

The Wormy Spaghetti

The next day, to pay Mr Twit back for the frog trick, Mrs Twit sneaked out into the garden and dug up some worms. She chose big long ones and put them in a tin and carried the tin back to the house under her apron.

At one o'clock, she cooked spaghetti for lunch and she mixed the worms in with the spaghetti, but only on her husband's plate. The worms didn't show because everything was covered with tomato sauce and sprinkled with cheese.

'Hey, my spaghetti's moving!' cried Mr Twit, poking around in it with his fork.

'It's a new kind,' Mrs Twit said, taking a mouthful from her own plate which of course had no worms. 'It's called Squiggly Spaghetti. It's delicious. Eat it up while it's nice and hot.'

Mr Twit started eating, twisting the long tomato-covered strings around his fork and shovelling them into his mouth. Soon there was tomato sauce all over his hairy chin.

'It's not as good as the ordinary kind,' he said, talking with his mouth full. 'It's too squishy.'

'I find it very tasty,' Mrs Twit said. She was watching him from the other end of the table. It gave her great pleasure to watch him eating worms.

'I find it rather bitter,' Mr Twit said. 'It's got a distinctly bitter flavour. Buy the other kind next time.'

Mrs Twit waited until Mr Twit had eaten the whole plateful. Then she said, 'You want to know why your spaghetti was squishy?'

Mr Twit wiped the tomato sauce from his beard with a corner of the tablecloth. 'Why?' he said.

'And why it had a nasty bitter taste?'

'Why?' he said.

'Because it was *worms*!' cried Mrs Twit, clapping her hands and stamping her feet on the floor and rocking with horrible laughter.

Chapter Eight

The Funny Walking-stick

To pay Mrs Twit back for the worms in his spaghetti, Mr Twit thought up a really clever nasty trick.

One night, when the old woman was asleep, he crept out of bed and took her walking-stick downstairs to his workshed. There he stuck a tiny round piece of wood (no thicker than a penny) on to the bottom of the stick.

This made the stick longer, but the difference was so small, the next morning Mrs Twit didn't notice it.

The following night, Mr Twit stuck on another tiny bit of wood. Every night, he crept downstairs and added an extra tiny thickness of wood to the end of the walking-stick. He did it very neatly so that the extra bits looked like a part of the old stick.

Gradually, but oh so gradually, Mrs Twit's walking-stick was getting longer and longer.

Now when something is growing very slowly, it is almost impossible to notice it happening. You yourself, for example, are actually growing taller every day that goes by, but you wouldn't think it, would you? It's happening so slowly you can't even notice it from one week to the next.

It was the same with Mrs Twit's walking-stick. It was all so slow and gradual that she didn't notice how long it was getting even when it was halfway up to her shoulder.

'That stick's too long for you,' Mr Twit said to her one day.

'Why so it is!' Mrs Twit said, looking at the stick. 'I've had a feeling there was something wrong but I couldn't for the life of me think what it was.'

'There's something wrong all right,' Mr Twit said, beginning to enjoy himself.

'What *can* have happened?' Mrs Twit said, staring at her old walking-stick. 'It must suddenly have grown longer.'

'Don't be a fool!' Mr Twit said. 'How can a walking-stick possibly grow longer? It's made of dead wood, isn't it? Dead wood can't grow.'

'Then what on earth has happened?' cried Mrs Twit.

'It's not the stick, it's *you*!' said Mr Twit, grinning horribly. 'It's *you* that's getting *shorter*! I've been noticing it for some time now.'

'That's not true!' cried Mrs Twit.

'You're shrinking, woman!' said Mr Twit.

'It's not possible!'

'Oh yes it jolly well is,' said Mr Twit. 'You're shrinking fast! You're shrinking *dangerously* fast! Why, you must have shrunk at least a foot in the last few days!'

'Never!' she cried.

'Of course you have! Take a look at your stick, you old goat, and see how much you've shrunk in comparison! You've got the *shrinks*, that's what you've got! You've got the dreaded *shrinks*!'

Mrs Twit began to feel so trembly she had to sit down.

Chapter Nine

Mrs Twit Has the Shrinks

As soon as Mrs Twit sat down, Mr Twit pointed at her and shouted, 'There you are! You're sitting in your old chair and you've shrunk so much your feet aren't even touching the ground!'

Mrs Twit looked down at her feet and by golly the man was right. Her feet were not touching the ground.

Mr Twit, you see, had been just as clever with the chair as he'd been with the walking-stick. Every night when he had gone downstairs and stuck a little bit extra on to the stick, he had done the same to the four legs of Mrs Twit's chair.

'Just look at you sitting there in your same old chair,' he cried, 'and you've shrunk so much your feet are dangling in the air!'

Mrs Twit went white with fear.

'You've got the *shrinks*!' cried Mr Twit, pointing his finger at her like a pistol. 'You've got them badly! You've got the most terrible case of shrinks I've ever seen!'

Mrs Twit became so frightened she began to dribble. But Mr Twit, still remembering the worms in his spaghetti, didn't feel sorry for her at all. 'I suppose you know what *happens* to you when you get the shrinks?' he said.

'What?' gasped Mrs Twit. 'What happens?'

'Your head SHRINKS into your neck . . .

'And your neck SHRINKS into your body . . .

'And your body SHRINKS into your legs . . .

'And your legs SHRINK into your feet. And in the end there's nothing left except a pair of shoes and a bundle of old clothes.'

'I can't bear it!' cried Mrs Twit.

'It's a terrible disease,' said Mr Twit. 'The worst in the world.'

'How long have I got?' cried Mrs Twit. 'How long before I finish up as a bundle of old clothes and a pair of shoes?'

Mr Twit put on a very solemn face. 'At the rate you're going,' he said, shaking his head sadly, 'I'd say not more than ten or eleven days.'

'But isn't there *anything* we can do?' cried Mrs Twit.

'There's only one cure for the shrinks,' said Mr Twit.

'Tell me!' she cried. 'Oh, tell me quickly!'

'We'll have to hurry!' said Mr Twit.

'I'm ready. I'll hurry! I'll do anything you say!' cried Mrs Twit.

'You won't last long if you don't,' said Mr Twit, giving her another grizzly grin.

'What is it I must do?' cried Mrs Twit, clutching her cheeks.

'You've got to be *stretched*,' said Mr Twit.

Chapter Ten

Mrs Twit Gets a Stretching

Mr Twit led Mrs Twit outdoors where he had everything ready for the great stretching.

He had one hundred balloons and lots of string.

He had a gas cylinder for filling the balloons.

He had fixed an iron ring into the ground.

'Stand here,' he said, pointing to the iron ring. He then tied Mrs Twit's ankles to the iron ring.

When that was done, he began filling the balloons with gas. Each balloon was on a long string and when it was filled with gas it pulled on its string, trying to go up and up. Mr Twit tied the ends of the strings to the top half of Mrs Twit's body. Some he tied round her neck, some under her arms, some to her wrists and some even to her hair.

Soon there were fifty coloured balloons floating in the air above Mrs Twit's head.

'Can you feel them stretching you?' asked Mr Twit.

'I can! I can!' cried Mrs Twit. 'They're stretching me like mad.'

He put on another ten balloons. The upward pull became very strong.

Mrs Twit was quite helpless now. With her feet tied to the ground and her arms pulled upwards by the balloons, she was unable to move. She was a prisoner, and Mr Twit had intended to go away and leave her like that for a couple of days and nights to teach her a lesson. In fact, he was just

about to leave when Mrs Twit opened her big mouth and said something silly.

'Are you sure my feet are tied properly to the ground?' she gasped. 'If those strings around my ankles break, it'll be goodbye for me!'

And that's what gave Mr Twit his second nasty idea.

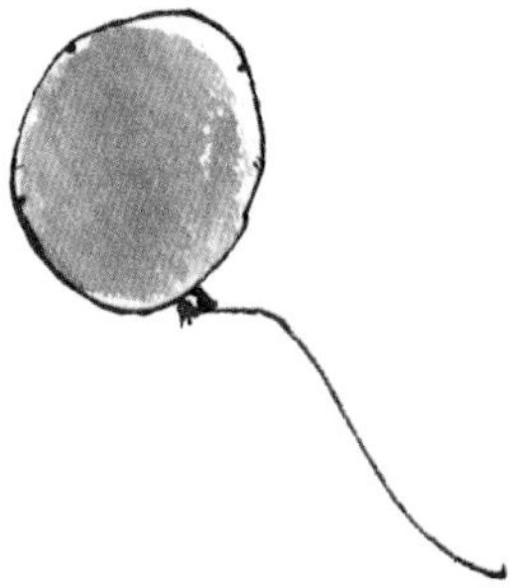

Chapter Eleven

Mrs Twit Goes Ballooning Up

'There's enough pull here to take me to the moon!' Mrs Twit cried out.

'To take you to *the moon*!' exclaimed Mr Twit. 'What a ghastly thought! We wouldn't want anything like that to happen, oh dear me no!'

'We most certainly wouldn't!' cried Mrs Twit. 'Put some more string around my ankles quickly! I want to feel absolutely safe!'

'Very well, my angel,' said Mr Twit, and with a ghoulish grin on his lips he knelt down at her feet. He took a knife from his pocket and with one quick slash he cut through the strings holding Mrs Twit's ankles to the iron ring.

She went up like a rocket.

'Help!' she screamed. 'Save me!'

But there was no saving her now. In a few seconds she was high up in the blue sky and climbing fast.

Mr Twit stood below looking up. '*What* a pretty sight!' he said to himself. 'How lovely all those balloons look in the sky! And what a marvellous bit of luck for me! At last the old hag is lost and gone for ever.'

Chapter Twelve

Mrs Twit Comes Ballooning Down

Mrs Twit may have been ugly and she may have been beastly, but she was not stupid.

High up there in the sky, she had a bright idea. 'If I can get rid of some of these balloons,' she said to herself, 'I will stop going up and start to come down.'

She began biting through the strings that held the balloons to her wrists and arms and neck and hair. Each time she bit through a string and let the balloon float away, the upward pull got less and her rate of climb slowed down.

When she had bitten through twenty strings, she stopped going up altogether. She stayed still in the air.

She bit through one more string.

Very, very slowly, she began to float downwards.

It was a calm day. There was no wind at all. And because of this, Mrs Twit had gone absolutely straight up. She now began to come absolutely straight down.

As she floated gently down, Mrs Twit's petticoat billowed out like a parachute, showing her long knickers. It was a grand sight on a glorious day, and thousands of birds came flying in from miles around to stare at this extraordinary old woman in the sky.

Chapter Thirteen

Mr Twit Gets a Horrid Shock

Mr Twit, who thought he had seen his ugly wife for the last time, was sitting in the garden celebrating with a mug of beer.

Silently, Mrs Twit came floating down. When she was about the height of the house above Mr Twit, she suddenly called out at the top of her voice, 'Here I come, you grizzly old grunion! You rotten old turnip! You filthy old frumpet!'

Mr Twit jumped as though he'd been stung by a giant wasp. He dropped his beer. He looked up. He gaped. He gasped. He gurgled. A few choking sounds came out of his mouth. '*Ughhhhhhhh!*' he said. '*Arghhhhhhhh! Ouchhhhhhhh!*'

'I'll get you for this!' shouted Mrs Twit. She was floating down right on top of him. She was purple with rage and slashing the air with her long walking-stick which she had somehow managed to hang on to all the time. 'I'll swish you to a swazzle!' she shouted. 'I'll swash you to a swizzle! I'll gnash you to a gnozzle! I'll gnosh you to a gnazzle!' And before Mr Twit had time to run away, this bundle of balloons and petticoats and fiery fury landed right on top of him, lashing out with the stick and cracking him all over his body.

Chapter Fourteen

THE HOUSE, THE TREE AND THE MONKEY CAGE

But that's enough of that. We can't go on forever watching these two disgusting people doing disgusting things to each other. We must get ahead with the story.

Here is a picture of Mr and Mrs Twit's house and garden. Some house! It looks like a prison. And not a window anywhere.

‘Who wants windows?’ Mr Twit had said when they were building it. ‘Who wants every Tom, Dick and Harry peeping in to see what you’re doing?’ It didn’t occur to Mr Twit that windows were meant mainly for looking out of, not for looking into.

And what do you think of that ghastly garden? Mrs Twit was the gardener. She was very good at growing thistles and stinging-nettles. 'I always grow plenty of spiky thistles and plenty of stinging-nettles,' she used to say. 'They keep out nasty nosey little children.'

Near the house you can see Mr Twit's workshed.

To one side there is The Big Dead Tree. It never has any leaves on it because it's dead.

And not far from the tree, you can see the monkey cage. There are four monkeys in it. They belong to Mr Twit. You will hear about them later.

Chapter Fifteen

HUGTIGHT STICKY GLUE

Once a week, on Wednesdays, the Twits had Bird Pie for supper. Mr Twit caught the birds and Mrs Twit cooked them.

Mr Twit was good at catching birds. On the day before Bird Pie day, he would put the ladder up against The Big Dead Tree and climb into the branches with a bucket of glue and a paint-brush. The glue he used was something called HUGTIGHT and it was stickier than any other glue in the world. He would paint it along the tops of all the branches and then go away.

As the sun went down, birds would fly in from all around to roost for the night in The Big Dead Tree. They didn't know, poor things, that the branches were all smeared with horrible HUGTIGHT.

The moment they landed on a branch, their feet stuck and that was that.

The next morning, which was Bird Pie day, Mr Twit would climb up the ladder again and grab all the wretched birds that were stuck to the tree. It didn't matter what kind they were – song thrushes, blackbirds, sparrows, crows, little jenny wrens, robins, anything – they all went into the pot for Wednesday's Bird Pie supper.

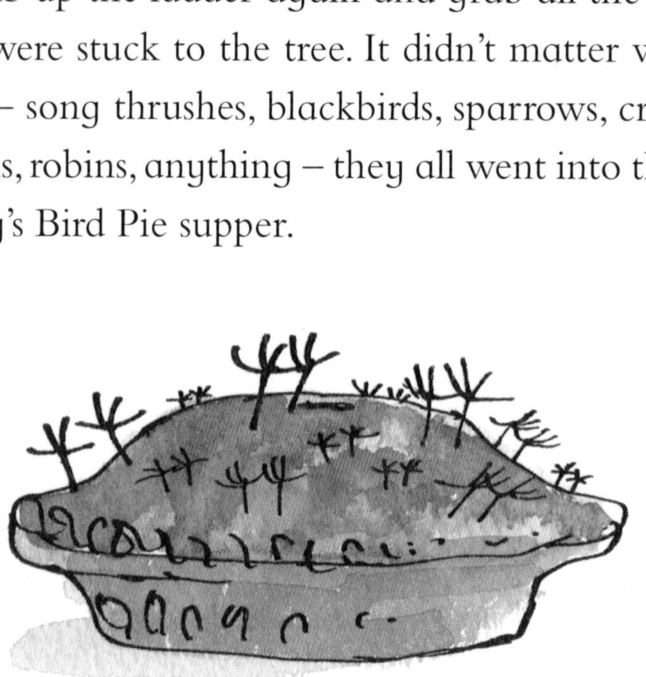

Chapter Sixteen

Four Sticky Little Boys

On one Tuesday evening after Mr Twit had been up the ladder and smeared the tree with HUGTIGHT, four little boys crept into the garden to look at the monkeys. They didn't care about the thistles and stinging-nettles, not when there were monkeys to look at. After a while, they got tired of looking at the monkeys, so they explored further into the garden and found the ladder leaning against The Big Dead Tree. They decided to climb up it just for fun.

There's nothing wrong with that.

The next morning, when Mr Twit went out to collect the birds, he found four miserable little boys sitting in the tree, stuck as tight as could be by the seats of their pants to the branches. There were no birds because the presence of the boys had scared them away.

Mr Twit was furious. 'As there are no birds for my pie tonight,' he shouted, 'then it'll have to be *boys* instead!'

He started to climb the ladder. 'Boy Pie might be better than Bird Pie,' he went on, grinning horribly. 'More meat and not so many tiny little bones!'

The boys were terrified. 'He's going to boil us!' cried one of them.

'He'll stew us alive!' wailed the second one.

'He'll cook us with carrots!' cried the third.

But the fourth little boy, who had more sense than the others, whispered, 'Listen, I've just had an idea. We are only stuck by *the seats of our pants*. So quick! Unbutton your pants and slip out of them and fall to the ground.'

Mr Twit had reached the top of the ladder and was just about to make a grab for the nearest boy when they all suddenly tumbled out of the tree and ran for home with their naked bottoms winking at the sun.

Chapter Seventeen

The Great Upside Down Monkey Circus

Now for the monkeys.

The four monkeys in the cage in the garden were all one family. They were Muggle-Wump and his wife and their two small children.

But what on earth were Mr and Mrs Twit doing with monkeys in their garden?

Well, in the old days, they had both worked in a circus as monkey trainers. They used to teach monkeys to do tricks and to dress up in human clothes and to smoke pipes and all the rest of that nonsense.

Today, although they were retired, Mr Twit still wanted to train monkeys. It was his dream that one day he would own the first GREAT UPSIDE DOWN MONKEY CIRCUS in the world.

That meant that the monkeys had to do everything upside down. They had to dance upside down (on their hands with their feet in the air). They had to play football upside down. They had to balance one on top of the other upside down, with Muggle-Wump at the bottom and the smallest baby monkey at the very top. They even had to eat and drink upside down and that is not an easy thing to do because the food and water has to go *up* your throat instead of down it. In fact, it is almost impossible, but the monkeys simply had to do it otherwise they got nothing.

All this sounds pretty silly to you and me. It sounded pretty silly to the monkeys, too. They absolutely hated having to do this upside down nonsense day after day. It made them giddy standing on their heads for hours on end. Sometimes the two small monkey children would faint with so much blood going to their heads. But Mr Twit didn't care about that. He kept them practising for six hours every day and if they didn't do as they were told, Mrs Twit would soon come running with her beastly stick.

Chapter Eighteen

The Roly-Poly Bird to the Rescue

Muggle-Wump and his family longed to escape from the cage in Mr Twit's garden and go back to the African jungle where they came from.

They hated Mr and Mrs Twit for making their lives so miserable.

They also hated them for what they did to the birds every Tuesday and Wednesday. 'Fly away, birds!' they used to shout, jumping about in the cage and waving their arms. 'Don't sit on that Big Dead Tree! It's just been smeared all over with sticky glue! Go and sit somewhere else!'

But these were English birds and they couldn't understand the weird African language the monkeys spoke. So they took no notice and went on using The Big Dead Tree and getting caught for Mrs Twit's Bird Pie.

Then one day, a truly magnificent bird flew down out of the sky and landed on the monkey cage.

'Good heavens!' cried all the monkeys together. 'It's the Roly-Poly Bird! What on earth are you doing over here in England, Roly-Poly Bird?' Like the monkeys, the Roly-Poly Bird came from Africa and he spoke the same language as they did.

'I've come for a holiday,' said the Roly-Poly Bird. 'I like to travel.' He fluffed his marvellous coloured feathers and looked down rather grandly at the monkeys. 'For most people,' he went on, 'flying away on holiday is very expensive, but I can fly anywhere in the world for nothing.'

'Do you know how to talk to these English birds?' Muggle-Wump asked him.

'Of course I do,' said the Roly-Poly Bird. 'It's no good going to a country and not knowing the language.'

'Then we must hurry,' said Muggle-Wump. 'Today is Tuesday and over there you can already see the revolting Mr Twit up the ladder painting sticky glue on all the branches of The Big Dead Tree. This evening when the birds come in to roost, you must warn them not to perch on that tree or they will be made into Bird Pie.'

That evening, the Roly-Poly Bird flew round and round The Big Dead Tree singing out,

'There's sticky stick stuff all over the tree!
If you land in the branches, you'll never get free!
So fly away! Fly away! Stay up high!
Or you'll finish up tomorrow in a hot Bird Pie!'

Chapter Nineteen

No Bird Pie for Mr Twit

The next morning when Mr Twit came out with his huge basket to snatch all the birds from The Big Dead Tree, there wasn't a single one on it. They were all sitting on top of the monkey cage. The Roly-Poly Bird was there as well, and Muggle-Wump and his family were inside the cage and the whole lot of them were laughing at Mr Twit.

Chapter Twenty

STILL NO BIRD PIE FOR MR TWIT

Mr Twit wasn't going to wait another week for his Bird Pie supper. He loved Bird Pie. It was his favourite meal. So that very same day, he went after the birds again. This time he smeared all the top bars of the monkey cage with sticky glue, as well as the branches of The Big Dead Tree. 'Now I'll get you,' he said, 'whichever one you sit on!'

The monkeys crouched inside the cage watching all this, and later on, when the Roly-Poly Bird came swooping in for an evening chat, they shouted out, 'Don't land on our cage, Roly-Poly Bird! It's covered in sticky glue! So is the tree!'

And that evening, as the sun went down and all the birds came in again to roost, the Roly-Poly Bird flew round and round the monkey cage and The Big Dead Tree, singing out his warning,

'There's sticky stuff now on the cage *and* the tree!
If you land on either, you'll never get free!
So fly away! Fly away! Stay up high!
Or you'll finish up tomorrow in a hot Bird Pie!'

Chapter Twenty-one

Mr and Mrs Twit Go Off to Buy Guns

The next morning when Mr Twit came out with his huge basket, not a single bird was sitting on either the monkey cage or The Big Dead Tree. They were all perched happily on the roof of Mr Twit's house. The Roly-Poly Bird was up there as well, and the monkeys were in the cage and the whole lot of them were hooting with laughter at Mr Twit.

'I'll wipe that silly laugh off your beaks!' Mr Twit screamed at the birds. 'I'll get you next time, you filthy feathery frumps! I'll wring your necks, the whole lot of you, and have you bubbling in the pot for Bird Pie before this day is out!'

'How are you going to do that?' asked Mrs Twit, who had come outside to see what all the noise was about. 'I won't have you smearing sticky glue all over the roof of our house!'

Mr Twit got very excited. 'I've got a great idea!' he cried. He didn't bother to keep his voice down because he didn't think the monkeys could understand. 'We'll both go into town right away and we'll buy a gun each!' he shouted. 'How's that?'

'Brilliant!' cried Mrs Twit, grinning and showing her long yellow teeth. 'We'll buy those big shotguns that spray out fifty bullets or more with each bang!'

'Exactly,' said Mr Twit. 'Lock up the house while I go and make sure the monkeys are safely shut away.'

Mr Twit went over to the monkey cage. 'Attention!' he barked in his fearsome monkey-trainer's voice. 'Upside down all of you and jump to it! One on top of the other! Quick! Get on with it or you'll feel Mrs Twit's stick across your backsides!'

Obediently, the poor monkeys stood on their hands and clambered one on top of the other, with Muggle-Wump at the bottom and the smallest child at the very top.

'Now stay there till we come back!' Mr Twit ordered. 'Don't you dare to move! And don't overbalance! When we return in two or three hours' time, I shall expect to find you all in exactly the same position as you are now! You understand?'

With that, Mr Twit marched away. Mrs Twit went with him. And the monkeys were left alone with the birds.

Chapter Twenty-two

Muggle-Wump Has an Idea

As soon as Mr and Mrs Twit had disappeared down the road, the monkeys all flipped back on to their feet the right way up. 'Quick, get the key!' Muggle-Wump called out to the Roly-Poly Bird, who was still sitting on the roof of the house.

'What key?' shouted the Roly-Poly Bird.

'The key to the door of our cage,' cried Muggle-Wump. 'It's hanging on a nail in the workshed. That's where he always puts it.'

The Roly-Poly Bird flew down and came back with the key in his beak. Muggle-Wump reached a hand through the bars of the cage and took the key. He put it in the lock and turned it. The door opened. All four monkeys leapt out together.

'We are free!' cried the two little ones. 'Where shall we go, Dad? Where shall we hide?'

'Don't get excited,' said Muggle-Wump. 'Calm down, everybody. Before we escape from this beastly place we have one very important thing to do.'

'What?' they asked him.

'We're going to turn those terrible Twits UPSIDE DOWN!'

'We're going to *what*?' they cried. 'You must be joking, Dad!'

'I'm not joking,' Muggle-Wump said. 'We're going to turn both Mr and Mrs Twit UPSIDE DOWN with their legs in the air!'

'Don't be ridiculous,' the Roly-Poly Bird said. 'How can we possibly turn those two maggoty old monsters upside down?'

'We can, we can!' cried Muggle-Wump. 'We are going to make them stand on their heads for hours and hours! Perhaps for ever! Let *them* see what it feels like for a change!'

'How?' said the Roly-Poly Bird. 'Just tell me how.'

Muggle-Wump laid his head on one side and a tiny twinkling little smile touched the corners of his mouth. 'Now and again,' he said, 'but not very often, I have a brilliant idea. This is one of them. Follow me, my friends, follow me.' He scampered off towards the house and the three other monkeys and the Roly-Poly Bird went after him.

'Buckets and paint-brushes!' cried Muggle-Wump. 'That's what we want next! There are plenty in the workshed! Hurry up, everyone! Get a bucket and a paint-brush!'

Inside Mr Twit's workshed there was an enormous barrel of HUGTIGHT sticky glue, the stuff he used for catching birds. 'Fill your buckets!' Muggle-Wump ordered. 'We are now going into the big house!'

Mrs Twit had hidden the key to the front door under the mat and Muggle-Wump had seen her doing it, so it was easy for them to get in. In they went, all four monkeys, with their buckets of sticky glue. Then came the Roly-Poly Bird flying in after them, with a bucket in his beak and a brush in his claw.

Chapter Twenty-three

The Great Glue Painting Begins

'This is the living-room,' announced Muggle-Wump. 'The grand and glorious living-room where those two fearful frumptious freaks eat Bird Pie every week for supper!'

'Please don't mention Bird Pie again,' said the Roly-Poly Bird. 'It gives me the shudders.'

'We mustn't waste time!' cried Muggle-Wump. 'Hurry up, hurry up! Now the first thing is this! I want everyone to paint sticky glue all over the ceiling! Cover it all! Smear it in every corner!'

'Over the ceiling!' they cried. 'Why the *ceiling*?'

'Never mind why!' shouted Muggle-Wump. 'Just do as you're told and don't argue!'

'But how do we get *up* there?' they asked. 'We can't reach.'

'Monkeys can reach anywhere!' shouted Muggle-Wump. He was in a frenzy of excitement now, waving his paint-brush and his bucket and leaping about all over the room. 'Come on, come on! Jump on the table! Stand on the chairs! Hop on each other's shoulders! Roly-Poly can do it flying! Don't stand there gaping! We have to hurry, don't you understand that? Those terrible Twits will be back any moment and this time they'll have *guns*! Get on with it, for heaven's sake! Get on with it!'

And so the great glue painting of the ceiling began. All the other birds who had been sitting on the roof flew in to help, carrying paint-brushes in their claws and beaks. There were buzzards, magpies, rooks, ravens and many more. Everyone was splashing away like mad and, with so many helpers, the job was soon finished.

Chapter Twenty-four

The Carpet Goes on the Ceiling

'What now?' they all said, looking at Muggle-Wump.

'Ah-ha!' cried Muggle-Wump. 'Now for the fun! Now for the greatest upside down trick of all time! Are you ready?'

'We're ready,' said the monkeys. 'We're ready,' said the birds.

'Pull out the carpet!' shouted Muggle-Wump. 'Pull this huge carpet out from under the furniture and stick it on to the ceiling!'

'On to the *ceiling*!' cried one of the small monkeys. 'But that's impossible, Dad!'

'I'll stick *you* on to the ceiling if you don't shut up!' snapped Muggle-Wump.

'He's dotty!' they cried.

'He's balmy!'

'He's batty!'

'He's nutty!'

'He's screwy!'

'He's wacky!' cried the Roly-Poly Bird. 'Poor old Muggles has gone off his wump at last!'

'Oh, do stop shouting such rubbish and give me a hand,' said Muggle-Wump, catching hold of one corner of the carpet. 'Pull, you nitwits, pull!'

The carpet was enormous. It covered the entire floor from wall to wall. It had a red and gold pattern on it. It is not easy to pull an enormous carpet off the floor when the room is full of tables and chairs. 'Pull!' yelled Muggle-Wump. 'Pull, pull, pull!' He was like a demon hopping round the room and telling everyone what to do. But you couldn't blame him. After months and months of standing on his head with his family, he couldn't wait for the time when the terrible Twits would be doing the same thing. At least that's what he hoped.

With the monkey and the birds all pulling and puffing, the carpet was dragged off the floor and finally hoisted up on the ceiling. And there it stuck.

All at once, the whole ceiling of the living-room was carpeted in red and gold.

Chapter Twenty-five

The Furniture Goes Up

'Now the table, the big table!' shouted Muggle-Wump. 'Turn the table upside down and put a dollop of sticky glue on to the bottom of each leg. Then we shall stick that on to the ceiling as well!'

Hoisting the huge table upside down on to the ceiling was not an easy job, but they managed it in the end.

'Will it stay there?' they cried. 'Is the glue strong enough to hold it up?'

'It's the strongest glue in the world!' Muggle-Wump replied. 'It's the special bird-catching bird-killing glue for smearing on trees!'

'Please,' said the Roly-Poly Bird. 'I have asked you before not to mention that subject. How would *you* like it if it was Monkey Pie they made every Wednesday and all your friends had been boiled up and I went on talking about it?'

'I do beg your pardon,' said Muggle-Wump. 'I'm so excited I hardly know what I'm saying. Now the chairs! Do the same with the chairs! All the chairs must be stuck upside down to the ceiling! And in their right places! Oh, do hurry up, everybody! Any moment now, those two filthy freaks are going to come rushing in with their guns!'

The monkeys, with the birds helping them, put glue on the bottom of each chair leg and hoisted them up to the ceiling.

'Now the smaller tables!' shouted Muggle-Wump. 'And the big sofa! And the sideboard! And the lamps! And all the tiny little things! The ashtrays! The ornaments! And that beastly plastic gnome on the sideboard! Everything, absolutely everything must be stuck to the ceiling!'

It was terribly hard work. It was especially difficult to stick everything on to the ceiling in exactly its right place. But they got it done in the end.

'What now?' asked the Roly-Poly Bird. He was out of breath and so tired he could hardly flap his wings.

'Now the pictures!' cried Muggle-Wump. 'Turn all the pictures upside down! And will one of you birds please fly out on to the road and watch to see when those frumptious freaks are coming back.'

'I'll go,' said the Roly-Poly Bird. 'I'll sit on the telephone wires and keep guard. It'll give me a rest.'

Chapter Twenty-six

The Ravens Swoop Over

They had only just finished the job when the Roly-Poly Bird came swooping in, screaming, 'They're coming back! They're coming back!'

Quickly, the birds flew back on to the roof of the house. The monkeys rushed into their cage and stood upside down one on top of the other. A moment later, Mr and Mrs Twit came marching into the garden, each carrying a fearsome-looking gun.

'I'm glad to see those monkeys are still upside down,' said Mr Twit.

'They're too stupid to do anything else,' said Mrs Twit. 'Hey, look at all those cheeky birds still up there on the roof! Let's go inside and load our lovely new guns and then it'll be *bang bang bang* and Bird Pie for supper.'

Just as Mr and Mrs Twit were about to enter the house, two black ravens swooped low over their heads. Each bird carried a paint-brush in its claw and each paint-brush was smeared with sticky glue. As the ravens whizzed over, they brushed a streak of sticky glue on to the tops of Mr and Mrs Twit's heads. They did it with the lightest touch but even so the Twits both felt it.

'What was *that*?' cried Mrs Twit. 'Some beastly bird has dropped his dirty droppings on my head!'

'On mine too!' shouted Mr Twit. 'I felt it! I felt it!'

'Don't touch it!' cried Mrs Twit. 'You'll get it all over your hands! Come inside and we'll wash it off at the sink!'

'The filthy dirty brutes,' yelled Mr Twit. 'I'll bet they did it on purpose! Just wait till I've loaded up my gun!'

Mrs Twit got the key from under the doormat (where Muggle-Wump had carefully replaced it) and into the house they went.

Chapter Twenty-seven

The Twits Are Turned Upside Down

'*What's this?*' gasped Mr Twit as they entered the living-room.

'*What's happened?*' screamed Mrs Twit.

They stood in the middle of the room, looking up. All the furniture, the big table, the chairs, the sofa, the lamps, the little side tables, the cabinet with bottles of beer in it, the ornaments, the electric fire, the carpet, everything was stuck upside down to the ceiling. The pictures were upside down on the walls.

And the floor they were standing on was absolutely bare. What's more, it had been painted white to look like the ceiling.

'*Look!*' screamed Mrs Twit. '*That's the floor! The floor's up there! This is the ceiling! We are standing on the ceiling!*'

'We're UPSIDE DOWN!' gasped Mr Twit. 'We *must* be upside down. We are standing on the ceiling looking down at the floor!'

'Oh help!' screamed Mrs Twit. 'Help help help! I'm beginning to feel giddy!'

'So am I! So am I!' cried Mr Twit. 'I don't like this one little bit!'

'We're upside down and all the blood's going to my head!' screamed Mrs Twit. 'If we don't do something quickly, I shall die, I know I will!'

'I've got it!' cried Mr Twit. 'I know what we'll do! *We'll stand on our heads, then anyway we'll be the right way up!'*

So they stood on their heads, and of course, the moment the tops of their heads touched the floor, the sticky glue that the ravens had brushed on a few moments before did its job. They were stuck. They were pinned down, cemented, glued, fixed to the floorboards.

Through a crack in the door the monkeys watched. They'd jumped right out of their cage the moment the Twits had gone inside. And the Roly-Poly Bird watched. And all the other birds flew in and out to catch a glimpse of this extraordinary sight.

Chapter Twenty-eight

The Monkeys Escape

That evening, Muggle-Wump and his family went up to the big wood on top of the hill, and in the tallest tree of all they built a marvellous treehouse. All the birds, especially the big ones, the crows and rooks and magpies, made their nests around the treehouse so that nobody could see it from the ground.

'You can't stay up here for ever, you know,' the Roly-Poly Bird said.

'Why not?' asked Muggle-Wump. 'It's a lovely place.'

'Just you wait till the winter comes,' the Roly-Poly Bird said. 'Monkeys don't like cold weather, do they?'

'They most certainly don't!' cried Muggle-Wump. 'Are the winters so very cold over here?'

'It's all snow and ice,' said the Roly-Poly Bird. 'Sometimes it's so cold a bird will wake up in the morning with his feet frozen to the bough that he's been roosting on.'

'Then what shall we do?' cried Muggle-Wump. 'My family will all be deep-freezed!'

'No, they won't,' said the Roly-Poly Bird. 'Because when the first leaves start falling from the trees in the autumn, you can all fly home to Africa with me.'

'Don't be ridiculous,' Muggle-Wump said. 'Monkeys can't fly.'

'You can sit on my back,' said the Roly-Poly Bird. 'I shall take you one at a time. You will travel by the Roly-Poly Super Jet and it won't cost you a penny!'

Chapter Twenty-nine

The Twits Get the Shrinks

And down here in the horrid house, Mr and Mrs Twit are still stuck upside down to the floor of the living-room.

'It's all your fault!' yelled Mr Twit, thrashing his legs in the air. '*You're* the one, you ugly old cow, who went hopping around shouting, "We're upside down! We're upside down!"'

'And *you're* the one who said to stand on our heads so we'd be the right way up, you whiskery old warthog!' screamed Mrs Twit. 'Now we'll never get free! We're stuck here for ever!'

'*You* may be stuck here for ever,' said Mr Twit. 'But not me! I'm going to get away!'

Mr Twit wriggled and squirmed, and he squiggled and wormed, and he twisted and turned, and he choggled and churned, but the sticky glue held him to the floor just as tightly as it had once held the poor birds in The Big Dead Tree. He was still as upside down as ever, standing on his head.

But heads are not made to be stood upon. If you stand on your head for a very long time, a horrid thing happens, and this was where Mr Twit got his biggest shock of all. With so much weight on it from up above, his head began to get squashed into his body.

Quite soon, it had disappeared completely, sunk out of sight in the fatty folds of his flabby neck.

'I'm SHRINKING!' burbled Mr Twit.

'So am I!' cried Mrs Twit.

'Help me! Save me! Call a doctor!' yelled Mr Twit. 'I'm getting THE DREADED SHRINKS!'

And so he was. Mrs Twit was getting THE DREADED SHRINKS, too! And this time it wasn't a fake. It was the real thing!

Their heads SHRANK into their necks . . .

Then their necks began SHRINKING into their bodies . . .

And their bodies began SHRINKING into their legs . . .

And their legs began SHRINKING into their feet . . .

And one week later, on a nice sunny afternoon, a man called Fred came round to read the gas meter. When nobody answered the door, Fred peeped into the house and there he saw, on the floor of the living-room, two bundles of old clothes, two pairs of shoes and a walking-stick. There was nothing more left in this world of Mr and Mrs Twit.

And everyone, including Fred, shouted . . . 'HOORAY!'

George's Marvellous Medicine

~ This book is for doctors everywhere ~

WARNING TO READERS:
Do not try to make George's Marvellous Medicine yourselves at home.
It could be dangerous.

Chapter One

GRANDMA

'I'm going shopping in the village,' George's mother said to George on Saturday morning. 'So be a good boy and don't get up to mischief.'

This was a silly thing to say to a small boy at any time. It immediately made him wonder what sort of mischief he might get up to.

'And don't forget to give Grandma her medicine at eleven o'clock,' the mother said. Then out she went, closing the back door behind her.

Grandma, who was dozing in her chair by the window, opened one wicked little eye and said, 'Now you heard what your mother said, George. Don't forget my medicine.'

'No, Grandma,' George said.

'And just try to behave yourself for once while she's away.'

'Yes, Grandma,' George said.

George was bored to tears. He didn't have a brother or a sister. His father was a farmer and the farm they lived on was miles away from anywhere, so there were never any children to play with. He was tired of staring at pigs and hens and cows and sheep. He was especially tired of having to live in the same house as that grizzly old grunion of a Grandma. Looking after her all by himself was hardly the most exciting way to spend a Saturday morning.

'You can make me a nice cup of tea for a start,' Grandma said to George. 'That'll keep you out of mischief for a few minutes.'

'Yes, Grandma,' George said.

George couldn't help disliking Grandma. She was a selfish grumpy old woman. She had pale brown teeth and a small puckered-up mouth like a dog's bottom.

'How much sugar in your tea today, Grandma?' George asked her.

'One spoon,' she said. 'And no milk.'

Most grandmothers are lovely, kind, helpful old ladies, but not this one. She spent all day and every day sitting in her chair by the window, and she was always complaining, grousing, grouching, grumbling, griping about something or other. Never once, even on her best days, had she smiled at George and said, 'Well, how are you this morning, George?' or 'Why don't you and I have a game of Snakes and Ladders?' or 'How was school today?' She didn't seem to care about other people, only about herself. She was a miserable old grouch.

George went into the kitchen and made Grandma a cup of tea with a teabag. He put one spoon of sugar in it and no milk. He stirred the sugar well and carried the cup into the living-room.

Grandma sipped the tea. 'It's not sweet enough,' she said. 'Put more sugar in.'

George took the cup back to the kitchen and added another spoonful of sugar. He stirred it again and carried it carefully in to Grandma.

'Where's the saucer?' she said. 'I won't have a cup without a saucer.'

George fetched her a saucer.

'And what about a teaspoon, if you please?'

'I've stirred it for you, Grandma. I stirred it well.'

'I'll stir my own tea, thank you very much,' she said. 'Fetch me a teaspoon.'

George fetched her a teaspoon.

When George's mother or father were home, Grandma never ordered George about like this. It was only when she had him on her own that she began treating him badly.

'You know what's the matter with you?' the old woman said, staring at George over the rim of the teacup with those bright wicked little eyes. 'You're *growing* too fast. Boys who grow too fast become stupid and lazy.'

'But I can't help it if I'm growing fast, Grandma,' George said.

'Of course you can,' she snapped. 'Growing's a nasty childish habit.'

'But we *have* to grow, Grandma. If we didn't grow, we'd never be grown-ups.'

'Rubbish, boy, rubbish,' she said. 'Look at me. Am I growing? Certainly not.'

'But you did once, Grandma.'

'Only *very little*,' the old woman answered. 'I gave up growing when I was extremely small, along with all the other nasty childish habits like laziness and disobedience and greed and sloppiness and untidiness and stupidity. You haven't given up any of these things, have you?'

'I'm still only a little boy, Grandma.'

'You're eight years old,' she snorted. 'That's old enough to know better. If you don't stop growing soon, it'll be too late.'

'Too late for what, Grandma?'

'It's ridiculous,' she went on. 'You're nearly as tall as me already.'

George took a good look at Grandma. She certainly was a *very tiny* person. Her legs were so short she had to have a footstool to put her feet on, and her head only came halfway up the back of the armchair.

'Daddy says it's fine for a man to be tall,' George said.

'Don't listen to your daddy,' Grandma said. 'Listen to me.'

'But how do I stop myself growing?' George asked her.

'Eat less chocolate,' Grandma said.

'Does chocolate make you grow?'

'It makes you grow the *wrong way*,' she snapped. 'Up instead of down.'

Grandma sipped some tea but never took her eyes from the little boy who stood before her. 'Never grow up,' she said. 'Always down.'

'Yes, Grandma.'

'And stop eating chocolate. Eat cabbage instead.'

'Cabbage! Oh no, I don't like cabbage,' George said.

'It's not what you like or what you don't like,' Grandma snapped. 'It's what's good for you that counts. From now on, you must eat cabbage three times a day. Mountains of cabbage! And if it's got caterpillars in it, so much the better!'

'Owch,' George said.

'Caterpillars give you brains,' the old woman said.

'Mummy washes them down the sink,' George said.

'Mummy's as stupid as you are,' Grandma said. 'Cabbage doesn't taste of anything without a few boiled caterpillars in it. Slugs, too.'

'Not *slugs*!' George cried out. 'I couldn't eat slugs!'

'Whenever I see a live slug on a piece of lettuce,' Grandma said, 'I gobble it up quick before it crawls away. Delicious.' She squeezed her lips together tight so that her mouth became a tiny wrinkled hole. 'Delicious,' she said again. 'Worms and slugs and beetley bugs. You don't know what's good for you.'

'You're joking, Grandma.'

'I never joke,' she said. 'Beetles are perhaps best of all. They go *crunch*!'

'Grandma! That's beastly!'

The old hag grinned, showing those pale brown teeth. 'Sometimes, if you're lucky,' she said, 'you get a beetle inside the stem of a stick of celery. That's what I like.'

'Grandma! How *could* you?'

'You find all sorts of nice things in sticks of raw celery,' the old woman went on. 'Sometimes it's earwigs.'

'I don't want to hear about it!' cried George.

'A big fat earwig is very tasty,' Grandma said, licking her lips. 'But you've got to be very quick, my dear, when you put one of those in your mouth. It has a pair of sharp nippers on its back end and if it grabs your tongue with those, it never lets go. So you've got to bite the earwig first, *chop chop*, before it bites you.'

George started edging towards the door. He wanted to get as far away as possible from this filthy old woman.

'You're trying to get away from me, aren't you?' she said, pointing a finger straight at George's face. 'You're trying to get away from Grandma.'

Little George stood by the door staring at the old hag in the chair. She stared back at him.

Could it be, George wondered, that she was a witch? He had always thought witches were only in fairy tales, but now he was not so sure.

'Come closer to me, little boy,' she said, beckoning to him with a horny finger. 'Come closer to me and I will tell you *secrets*.'

George didn't move.

Grandma didn't move either.

'I know a great many secrets,' she said, and suddenly she smiled. It was a thin icy smile, the kind a snake might make just before it bites you. 'Come over here to Grandma and she'll whisper secrets to you.'

George took a step backwards, edging closer to the door.

'You mustn't be frightened of your old Grandma,' she said, smiling that icy smile.

George took another step backwards.

'Some of us,' she said, and all at once she was leaning forward in her chair and whispering in a throaty sort of voice George had never heard her use before. 'Some of us,' she said, 'have magic powers that can twist the creatures of this earth into wondrous shapes . . .'

A tingle of electricity flashed down the length of George's spine. He began to feel frightened.

'Some of us,' the old woman went on, 'have fire on our tongues and sparks in our bellies and wizardry in the tips of our fingers . . .

'Some of us know secrets that would make your hair stand straight up on end and your eyes pop out of their sockets . . .'

George wanted to run away, but his feet seemed stuck to the floor.

'We know how to make your nails drop off and teeth grow out of your fingers instead.'

George began to tremble. It was her face that frightened him most of all, the frosty smile, the brilliant unblinking eyes.

'We know how to have you wake up in the morning with a long tail coming out from behind you.'

'Grandma!' he cried out. 'Stop!'

'We know secrets, my dear, about dark places where dark things live and squirm and slither all over each other . . .'

George made a dive for the door.

'It doesn't matter how far you run,' he heard her saying, 'you won't ever get away . . .'

George ran into the kitchen, slamming the door behind him.

Chapter Two

The Marvellous Plan

George sat himself down at the table in the kitchen. He was shaking a little. Oh, how he hated Grandma! He really *hated* that horrid old witchy woman. And all of a sudden he had a tremendous urge to *do something* about her. Something *whopping*. Something *absolutely terrific*. A *real shocker*. A sort of explosion. He wanted to blow away the witchy smell that hung about her in the next room. He may have been only eight years old but he was a brave little boy. He was ready to take this old woman on.

'I'm not going to be frightened by *her*,' he said softly to himself. But he *was* frightened. And that's why he wanted suddenly to explode her away.

Well . . . not quite away. But he did want to shake the old woman up a bit.

Very well, then. What should it be, this whopping terrific exploding shocker for Grandma?

He would have liked to put a firework banger under her chair but he didn't have one.

He would have liked to put a long green snake down the back of her dress but he didn't have a long green snake.

He would have liked to put six big black rats in the room with her and lock the door but he didn't have six big black rats.

As George sat there pondering this interesting problem, his eye fell upon the bottle of Grandma's brown medicine standing on the sideboard. Rotten stuff it seemed to be. Four times a day a large spoonful of it was shovelled into her mouth and it didn't

do her the slightest bit of good. She was always just as horrid after she'd had it as she'd been before. The whole point of medicine, surely, was to make a person better. If it didn't do that, then it was quite useless.

So-ho! thought George suddenly. *Ah-ha! Ho-hum!* I know exactly what I'll do. I shall make her a *new* medicine, one that is so strong and so fierce and so fantastic it will either cure her completely or blow off the top of her head. I'll make her a *magic medicine*, a medicine no doctor in the world has ever made before.

George looked at the kitchen clock. It said five past ten. There was nearly an hour left before Grandma's next dose was due at eleven.

'Here we go, then!' cried George, jumping up from the table. 'A magic medicine it shall be!'

'So give me a bug and a jumping flea,
Give me two snails and lizards three,
And a slimy squiggler from the sea,
And the poisonous sting of a bumblebee,
And the juice from the fruit of the ju-jube tree,
And the powdered bone of a wombat's knee.
And one hundred other things as well
Each with a rather nasty smell.
I'll stir them up, I'll boil them long,
A mixture tough, a mixture strong.
And then, heigh-ho, and down it goes,
A nice big spoonful (hold your nose)
Just gulp it down and have no fear.
"How do you like it, Granny dear?"
Will she go pop? Will she explode?
Will she go flying down the road?
Will she go poof in a puff of smoke?
Start fizzing like a can of Coke?
Who knows? Not I. Let's wait and see.
(I'm glad it's neither you nor me.)
Oh Grandma, if you only knew
What I have got in store for you!'

Chapter Three

George Begins to Make the Medicine

George took an enormous saucepan out of the cupboard and placed it on the kitchen table.

'George!' came the shrill voice from the next room. 'What are you doing?'

'Nothing, Grandma,' he called out.

'You needn't think I can't hear you just because you closed the door! You're rattling the saucepans!'

'I'm just tidying the kitchen, Grandma.'

Then there was silence.

George had absolutely no doubts whatsoever about how he was going to make his famous medicine. He wasn't going to fool about wondering whether to put in a little bit of this or a little bit of that. Quite simply, he was going to put in EVERYTHING he could find. There would be no messing about, no hesitating, no wondering whether a particular thing would knock the old girl sideways or not. The rule would be this: whatever he saw, if it was runny or powdery or gooey, in it went.

Nobody had ever made a medicine like that before. If it didn't actually cure Grandma, then it would anyway cause some exciting results. It would be worth watching.

George decided to work his way round the various rooms one at a time and see what they had to offer.

He would go first to the bathroom. There are always lots of

funny things in a bathroom. So upstairs he went, carrying the enormous two-handled saucepan before him.

In the bathroom, he gazed longingly at the famous and dreaded medicine cupboard. But he didn't go near it. It was the only thing in the entire house he was forbidden to touch. He had made solemn promises to his parents about this and he wasn't going to break them. There were things in there, they had told him, that could actually kill a person, and although he was out to give Grandma a pretty fiery mouthful, he didn't really want a dead body on his hands. George put the saucepan on the floor and went to work.

Number one was a bottle labelled GOLDEN GLOSS HAIR SHAMPOO. He emptied it into the pan. 'That ought to wash her tummy nice and clean,' he said.

He took a full tube of TOOTHPASTE and squeezed out the whole lot of it in one long worm. 'Maybe that will brighten up those horrid brown teeth of hers,' he said.

There was an aerosol can of SUPERFOAM SHAVING SOAP belonging to his father. George loved playing with aerosols. He pressed the button and kept his finger on it until there was nothing left. A wonderful mountain of white foam built up in the giant saucepan.

With his fingers, he scooped out the contents of a jar of VITAMIN ENRICHED FACE CREAM.

In went a small bottle of scarlet NAIL VARNISH. 'If the toothpaste doesn't clean her teeth,' George said, 'then this will paint them as red as roses.'

He found another jar of creamy stuff labelled HAIR REMOVER. SMEAR IT ON YOUR LEGS, it said, AND ALLOW TO REMAIN FOR FIVE MINUTES. George tipped it all into the saucepan.

There was a bottle with yellow stuff inside it called DISHWORTH'S FAMOUS DANDRUFF CURE. In it went.

There was something called BRILLIDENT FOR CLEANING FALSE TEETH. It was a white powder. In that went, too.

He found another aerosol can, NEVERMORE PONKING DEODORANT SPRAY, GUARANTEED, it said, TO KEEP AWAY UNPLEASANT BODY SMELLS FOR A WHOLE DAY. 'She could use plenty of that,' George said as he sprayed the entire canful into the saucepan.

LIQUID PARAFFIN, the next one was called. It was a big bottle. He hadn't the faintest idea what it did to you, but he poured it in anyway.

That, he thought, looking around him, was about all from the bathroom.

On his mother's dressing-table in the bedroom, George found yet another lovely aerosol can. It was called HELGA'S HAIRSET. HOLD TWELVE INCHES AWAY FROM THE HAIR AND SPRAY LIGHTLY. He squirted the whole lot into the saucepan. He *did* enjoy squirting these aerosols.

There was a bottle of perfume called FLOWERS OF TURNIPS. It smelled of old cheese. In it went.

And in, too, went a large round box of POWDER. It was called PINK PLASTER. There was a powder-puff on top and he threw that in as well for luck.

He found a couple of LIPSTICKS. He pulled the greasy red things out of their little cases and added them to the mixture.

The bedroom had nothing more to offer, so George carried the enormous saucepan downstairs again and trotted into the laundry-room where the shelves were full of all kinds of household items.

The first one he took down was a large box of SUPERWHITE FOR AUTOMATIC WASHING-MACHINES. DIRT, it said, WILL DISAPPEAR LIKE MAGIC. George didn't know whether Grandma was automatic or not, but she was certainly a dirty old woman. 'So she'd better have it all,' he said, tipping in the whole boxful.

Then there was a big tin of WAXWELL FLOOR POLISH. IT REMOVES FILTH AND FOUL MESSES FROM YOUR FLOOR AND LEAVES EVERYTHING SHINY BRIGHT, it said. George scooped the orange-coloured waxy stuff out of the tin and plonked it into the pan.

There was a round cardboard carton labelled FLEA POWDER FOR DOGS. KEEP WELL AWAY FROM THE DOG'S FOOD, it said, BECAUSE THIS POWDER, IF EATEN, WILL MAKE THE DOG EXPLODE. 'Good,' said George, pouring it all into the saucepan.

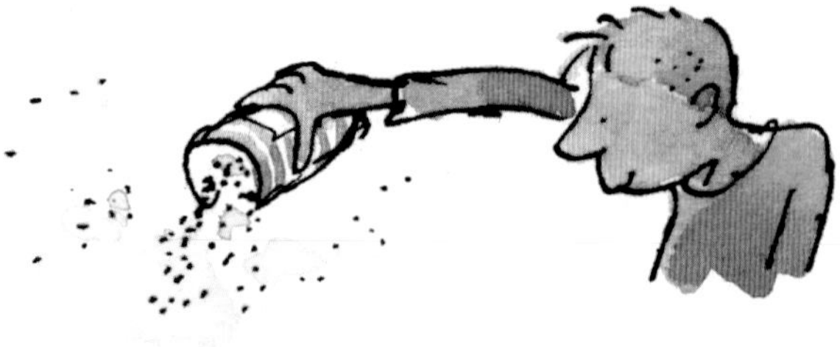

He found a box of CANARY SEED on the shelf. 'Perhaps it'll make the old bird sing,' he said, and in it went.

Next, George explored the box with shoe-cleaning materials – brushes and tins and dusters. Well now, he thought, Grandma's medicine is brown, so *my* medicine must also be brown or she'll smell a rat. The way to colour it, he decided, would be with BROWN SHOE-POLISH. The large tin he chose was labelled DARK TAN. Splendid. He scooped it all out with an old spoon and plopped it into the pan. He would stir it up later.

On his way back to the kitchen, George saw a bottle of GIN standing on the sideboard. Grandma was very fond of gin. She was allowed to have a small nip of it every evening. Now he would give her a treat. He would pour in the whole bottle. He did.

Back in the kitchen, George put the huge saucepan on the table and went over to the cupboard that served as a larder. The shelves were bulging with bottles and jars of every sort. He chose the following and emptied them one by one into the saucepan:

A TIN OF CURRY POWDER

A TIN OF MUSTARD POWDER

A BOTTLE OF 'EXTRA HOT' CHILLI SAUCE

A TIN OF BLACK PEPPERCORNS

A BOTTLE OF HORSERADISH SAUCE

'There!' he said aloud. 'That should do it!'

'George!' came the screechy voice from the next room. 'Who are you talking to in there? What are you up to?'

'Nothing, Grandma, absolutely nothing,' he called back.

'Is it time for my medicine yet?'

'No, Grandma, not for about half an hour.'

'Well, just see you don't forget it.'

'I won't, Grandma,' George answered. 'I promise I won't.'

Chapter Four

Animal Pills

At this point, George suddenly had an extra good wheeze. Although the medicine cupboard in the house was forbidden ground, what about the medicines his father kept on the shelf in the shed next to the henhouse? The animal medicines?

What about *those*?

Nobody had ever told him he mustn't touch *them*.

Let's face it, George said to himself, hair-spray and shaving-cream and shoe-polish are all very well and they will no doubt cause some splendid explosions inside the old geezer, but what the magic mixture now needs is a touch of the real stuff, real pills and real tonics, to give it punch and muscle.

George picked up the heavy three-quarters full saucepan and carried it out of the back door. He crossed the farmyard and headed straight for the shed alongside the henhouse. He knew his father wouldn't be there. He was out haymaking in one of the meadows.

George entered the dusty old shed and put the saucepan on the bench. Then he looked up at the medicine shelf. There were five big bottles there. Two were full of pills, two were full of runny stuff and one was full of powder.

'I'll use them all,' George said. 'Grandma needs them. Boy, does she need them!'

The first bottle he took down contained an orange-coloured powder. The label said, FOR CHICKENS WITH FOUL PEST, HEN GRIPE, SORE BEAKS, GAMMY LEGS, COCKERELITIS, EGG TROUBLE, BROODINESS OR LOSS OF FEATHERS. MIX ONE SPOONFUL ONLY WITH EACH BUCKET OF FEED.

'Well,' George said aloud to himself as he tipped in the whole bottleful, 'the old bird won't be losing any feathers after she's had a dose of this.'

The next bottle he took down had about five hundred gigantic purple pills in it.

FOR HORSES WITH HOARSE THROATS, it said on the label. THE HOARSE-THROATED HORSE SHOULD SUCK ONE PILL TWICE A DAY.

'Grandma may not have a hoarse throat,' George said, 'but she's certainly got a sharp tongue. Maybe they'll cure that instead.' Into the saucepan went the five hundred gigantic purple pills.

Then there was a bottle of thick yellowish liquid. FOR COWS, BULLS AND BULLOCKS, the label said. WILL CURE COW POX, COW MANGE, CRUMPLED HORNS, BAD BREATH IN BULLS, EARACHE, TOOTHACHE, HEADACHE, HOOF-ACHE, TAILACHE AND SORE UDDERS.

'That grumpy old cow in the living-room has every one of those rotten illnesses,' George said. 'She'll need it all.' With a slop and a gurgle, the yellow liquid splashed into the now nearly full saucepan.

The next bottle contained a brilliant red liquid. SHEEPDIP, it said on the label. FOR SHEEP WITH SHEEPROT AND FOR GETTING RID OF TICKS AND FLEAS. MIX ONE SPOONFUL IN ONE GALLON OF WATER AND SLOSH IT OVER THE SHEEP. CAUTION, DO NOT MAKE THE MIXTURE ANY STRONGER OR THE WOOL WILL FALL OUT AND THE ANIMAL WILL BE NAKED.

'By gum,' said George, 'how I'd love to walk in and slosh it all over old Grandma and watch the ticks and fleas go jumping off her. But I can't. I mustn't. So she'll have to drink it instead.' He poured the bright red medicine into the saucepan.

The last bottle on the shelf was full of pale green pills. PIG PILLS, the label announced. FOR PIGS WITH PORK PRICKLES, TENDER TROTTERS, BRISTLE BLIGHT AND SWINE SICKNESS. GIVE ONE PILL PER DAY. IN SEVERE CASES TWO PILLS MAY BE GIVEN, BUT MORE THAN THAT WILL MAKE THE PIG ROCK AND ROLL.

'Just the stuff,' said George, 'for that miserable old pig back there in the house. She'll need a very big dose.' He tipped all the green pills, hundreds and hundreds of them, into the saucepan.

There was an old stick lying on the bench that had been used for stirring paint. George picked it up and started to stir his marvellous concoction. The mixture was as thick as cream, and as he stirred and stirred, many wonderful colours rose up from the depths and blended together, pinks, blues, greens, yellows and browns.

George went on stirring until it was all well mixed, but even so there were still hundreds of pills lying on the bottom that hadn't melted. And there was his mother's splendid powder-puff floating on the surface. 'I shall have to boil it all up,' George said. 'One good quick boil on the stove is all it needs.' And with that he staggered back towards the house with the enormous heavy saucepan.

On the way, he passed the garage, so he went in to see if he could find any other interesting things. He added the following:

Half a pint of ENGINE OIL – to keep Grandma's engine going smoothly.

Some ANTI-FREEZE – to keep her radiator from freezing up in winter.

A handful of GREASE – to grease her creaking joints.

Then back to the kitchen.

Chapter Five

The Cook-up

In the kitchen, George put the saucepan on the stove and turned up the gas flame underneath it as high as it would go.

'George!' came the awful voice from the next room. 'It's time for my medicine!'

'Not yet, Grandma,' George called back. 'There's still twenty minutes before eleven o'clock.'

'What mischief are you up to in there now?' Granny screeched. 'I hear noises.'

George thought it best not to answer this one. He found a long wooden spoon in a kitchen drawer and began stirring hard. The stuff in the pot got hotter and hotter.

Soon the marvellous mixture began to froth and foam. A rich blue smoke, the colour of peacocks, rose from the surface of the liquid, and a fiery fearsome smell filled the kitchen. It made George choke and splutter. It was a smell unlike any he had smelled before. It was a brutal and bewitching smell, spicy and staggering, fierce and frenzied, full of wizardry and magic. Whenever he got a whiff of it up his nose, firecrackers went off in his skull and electric prickles ran along the backs of his legs.

It was wonderful to stand there stirring this amazing mixture and to watch it smoking blue and bubbling and frothing and foaming as though it were alive.

At one point, he could have sworn he saw bright sparks flashing in the swirling foam.

And suddenly, George found himself dancing around the steaming pot, chanting strange words that came into his head out of nowhere:

'Fiery broth and witch's brew
Foamy froth and riches blue
Fume and spume and spoondrift spray
Fizzle swizzle shout hooray
Watch it sloshing, swashing, sploshing
Hear it hissing, squishing, spissing
Grandma better start to pray.'

Chapter Six

Brown Paint

George turned off the heat under the saucepan. He must leave plenty of time for it to cool down.

When all the steam and froth had gone away, he peered into the giant pan to see what colour the great medicine now was. It was a deep and brilliant blue.

'It needs more brown in it,' George said. 'It simply must be brown or she'll get suspicious.'

George ran outside and dashed into his father's toolshed where all the paints were kept. There was a row of cans on the shelf, all colours, black, green, red, pink, white and brown. He reached for the can of brown. The label said simply DARK BROWN GLOSS PAINT ONE QUART. He took a screwdriver and prised off the lid. The can was three-quarters full. He rushed it back to the kitchen. He poured the whole lot into the saucepan. The saucepan was now full to the brim. Very gently, George stirred the paint into the mixture with the long wooden spoon. Ah-ha! It was all turning brown! A lovely rich creamy brown!

'Where's that medicine of mine, boy?!' came the voice from the living-room. 'You're forgetting me! You're doing it on purpose! I shall tell your mother!'

'I'm not forgetting you, Grandma,' George called back. 'I'm thinking of you all the time. But there are still ten minutes to go.'

'You're a nasty little maggot!' the voice screeched back. 'You're a lazy and disobedient little worm, and you're growing too fast.'

George fetched the bottle of Grandma's real medicine from

the sideboard. He took out the cork and tipped it all down the sink. He then filled the bottle with his own magic mixture by dipping a small jug into the saucepan and using it as a pourer.

He replaced the cork.

Had it cooled down enough yet? Not quite. He held the bottle under the cold tap for a couple of minutes. The label came off in the wet but that didn't matter. He dried the bottle with a dishcloth.

All was now ready!

This was it!

The great moment had arrived!

'Medicine time, Grandma!' he called out.

'I should hope so, too,' came the grumpy reply.

The silver tablespoon in which the medicine was always given lay ready on the kitchen sideboard. George picked it up.

Holding the spoon in one hand and the bottle in the other, he advanced into the living-room.

Chapter Seven

GRANDMA GETS THE MEDICINE

Grandma sat hunched in her chair by the window. The wicked little eyes followed George closely as he crossed the room towards her.

'You're late,' she snapped.

'I don't think I am, Grandma.'

'Don't interrupt me in the middle of a sentence!' she shouted.

'But you'd finished your sentence, Grandma.'

'There you go again!' she cried. 'Always interrupting and arguing. You really are a tiresome little boy. What's the time?'

'It's exactly eleven o'clock, Grandma.'

'You're lying as usual. Stop talking so much and give me my medicine. Shake the bottle first. Then pour it into the spoon and make sure it's a whole spoonful.'

'Are you going to gulp it all down in one go?' George asked her. 'Or will you sip it?'

'What I do is none of your business,' the old woman said. 'Fill the spoon.'

As George removed the cork and began very slowly to pour the thick brown stuff into the spoon, he couldn't help thinking back upon all the mad and marvellous things that had gone into the making of this crazy stuff – the shaving soap, the hair remover, the dandruff cure, the automatic washing-machine powder, the flea powder for dogs, the shoe-polish, the black pepper, the horseradish sauce and all the rest of them, not to mention the powerful animal pills and powders and liquids . . . and the brown paint.

'Open your mouth wide, Grandma,' he said, 'and I'll pop it in.'

The old hag opened her small wrinkled mouth, showing disgusting pale brown teeth.

'Here we go!' George cried out. 'Swallow it down!' He pushed the spoon well into her mouth and tipped the mixture down her throat. Then he stepped back to watch the result.

It was worth watching.

Grandma yelled '*Oweeeee!*' and her whole body shot up *whoosh* into the air. It was exactly as though someone had pushed an electric wire through the underneath of her chair and switched on the current. Up she went like a jack-in-the-box . . . and she didn't come down . . . she stayed there . . . suspended in mid-air . . . about two feet up . . . still in a sitting position . . .

but rigid now . . . frozen . . . quivering . . . the eyes bulging . . . the hair standing straight up on end.

'Is something wrong, Grandma?' George asked her politely. 'Are you all right?'

Suspended up there in space, the old girl was beyond speaking.

The shock that George's marvellous mixture had given her must have been tremendous.

You'd have thought she'd swallowed a red-hot poker the way she took off from that chair.

Then down she came again with a *plop*, back into her seat.

'Call the fire brigade!' she shouted suddenly. 'My stomach's on fire!'

'It's just the medicine, Grandma,' George said. 'It's good strong stuff.'

'Fire!' the old woman yelled. 'Fire in the basement! Get a bucket! Man the hoses! Do something quick!'

'Cool it, Grandma,' George said. But he got a bit of a shock when he saw the smoke coming out of her mouth and out of her nostrils. Clouds of black smoke were coming out of her nose and blowing around the room.

'By golly, you really are on fire,' George said.

'Of course I'm on fire!' she yelled. 'I'll be burned to a crisp! I'll be fried to a frizzle! I'll be boiled like a beetroot!'

George ran into the kitchen and came back with a jug of water. 'Open your mouth, Grandma!' he cried. He could hardly see her for the smoke, but he managed to pour half a jugful down her throat. A sizzling sound, the kind you get if you hold a hot frying-pan under a cold tap, came up from deep down in Grandma's stomach. The old hag bucked and shied and snorted. She gasped and gurgled. Spouts of water came shooting out of her. And the smoke cleared away.

'The fire's out,' George announced proudly. 'You'll be all right now, Grandma.'

'*All right?*' she yelled. 'Who's *all right*? There's jacky-jumpers in my tummy! There's squigglers in my belly! There's bangers in my bottom!' She began bouncing up and down in the chair. Quite obviously she was not very comfortable.

'You'll find it's doing you a lot of good, that medicine, Grandma,' George said.

'*Good?*' she screamed. 'Doing me *good*? It's *killing* me!'

Then she began to bulge.

She was swelling!

She was puffing up all over!

Someone was pumping her up, that's how it looked!

Was she going to explode?

Her face was turning from purple to green!

But wait! She had a puncture somewhere! George could hear the hiss of escaping air. She stopped swelling. She was going down. She was slowly getting thinner again, shrinking back and back slowly to her shrivelly old self.

'How's things, Grandma?' George said.

No answer.

Then a funny thing happened. Grandma's body gave a sudden sharp twist and a sudden sharp jerk and she flipped herself clear out of the chair and landed neatly on her two feet on the carpet.

'That's terrific, Grandma!' George cried. 'You haven't stood up like that for years! Look at you! You're standing up all on your own and you're not even using a stick!'

Grandma didn't even hear him. The frozen pop-eyed look was back with her again now. She was miles away in another world.

Marvellous medicine, George told himself. He found it fascinating to stand there watching what it was doing to the old hag. What next? he wondered.

He soon found out.

Suddenly she began to grow.

It was quite slow at first . . . just a very gradual inching upwards . . . up, up, up . . . inch by inch . . . getting taller and taller . . . about an inch every few seconds . . . and in the beginning George didn't notice it.

But when she had passed the five foot six mark and was going on up towards being six feet tall, George gave a jump and shouted, 'Hey, Grandma! You're *growing*! You're *going up*! Hang on, Grandma! You'd better stop now or you'll be hitting the ceiling!'

But Grandma didn't stop.

It was a truly fantastic sight, this ancient scrawny old woman getting taller and taller, longer and longer, thinner and thinner, as though she were a piece of elastic being pulled upwards by invisible hands.

When the top of her head actually touched the ceiling, George thought she was bound to stop.

But she didn't.

There was a sort of scrunching noise, and bits of plaster and cement came raining down.

'Hadn't you better stop now, Grandma?' George said. 'Daddy's just had this whole room repainted.'

But there was no stopping her now.

Soon, her head and shoulders had completely disappeared through the ceiling and she was still going.

George dashed upstairs to his own bedroom and there she was coming up through the floor like a mushroom.

'Whoopee!' she shouted, finding her voice at last. 'Hallelujah, here I come!'

'Steady on, Grandma,' George said.

'With a heigh-nonny-no and up we go!' she shouted. 'Just watch me grow!'

'This is *my* room,' George said. 'Look at the mess you're making.'

'Terrific medicine!' she cried. 'Give me some more!'

She's dotty as a doughnut, George thought.

'Come on, boy! Give me some more!' she yelled. 'Dish it out! I'm slowing down!'

George was still clutching the medicine bottle in one hand and the spoon in the other. Oh well, he thought, why not? He poured out a second dose and popped it into her mouth.

'*Oweee!*' she screamed and up she went again. Her feet were still on the floor downstairs in the living-room but her head was moving quickly towards the ceiling of the bedroom.

'I'm on my way now, boy!' she called down to George. 'Just watch me go!'

'That's the attic above you, Grandma!' George called out. 'I'd keep out of there! It's full of bugs and bogles!'

Crash! The old girl's head went through the ceiling as though it were butter.

George stood in his bedroom gazing at the shambles. There was a big hole in the floor and another in the ceiling, and sticking up like a post between the two was the middle part of Grandma. Her legs were in the room below, her head in the attic.

'I'm still going!' came the old screechy voice from up above. 'Give me another dose, my boy, and let's go through the roof!'

'No, Grandma, no!' George called back. 'You're busting up the whole house!'

'To heck with the house!' she shouted. 'I want some fresh air! I haven't been outside for twenty years!'

'By golly, she *is* going through the roof!' George told himself. He ran downstairs. He rushed out of the back door into the yard. It would be simply awful, he thought, if she bashed up the roof as well. His father would be furious. And he, George, would get the blame. *He* had made the medicine. *He* had given her too much. 'Don't come through the roof, Grandma,' he prayed. 'Please don't.'

Chapter Eight

The Brown Hen

George stood in the farmyard looking up at the roof. The old farmhouse had a fine roof of pale red tiles and tall chimneys.

There was no sign of Grandma. There was only a song-thrush sitting on one of the chimney-pots, singing a song. The old wurzel's got stuck in the attic, George thought. Thank goodness for that.

Suddenly a tile came clattering down from the roof and fell into the yard. The song-thrush took off fast and flew away.

Then another tile came down.

Then half a dozen more.

And then, very slowly, like some weird monster rising up from the deep, Grandma's head came through the roof . . .

Then her scrawny neck . . .

And the tops of her shoulders . . .

'How'm I doing, boy!' she shouted. 'How's that for a bash up?'

'Don't you think you'd better stop now, Grandma?' George called out . . .

'I have stopped!' she answered. 'I feel terrific! Didn't I tell you I had magic powers! Didn't I warn you I had wizardry in the tips of my fingers! But you wouldn't listen to me, would you? You wouldn't listen to your old Grandma!'

'*You* didn't do it, Grandma,' George shouted back to her. '*I* did it! I made you a new medicine!'

'*A new medicine? You?* What rubbish!' she yelled.

'I did! I did!' George shouted.

'You're lying as usual!' Grandma yelled. 'You're always lying!'

'I'm not lying, Grandma. I swear I'm not.'

The wrinkled old face high up on the roof stared down suspiciously at George. 'Are you telling me you actually made a new medicine all by yourself?' she shouted.

'Yes, Grandma, all by myself.'

'I don't believe you,' she answered. 'But I'm very comfortable up here. Fetch me a cup of tea.'

A brown hen was pecking about in the yard close to where George was standing. The hen gave him an idea. Quickly, he uncorked the medicine bottle and poured some of the brown stuff into the spoon. 'Watch this, Grandma!' he shouted. He crouched down, holding out the spoon to the hen.

'Chicken,' he said. 'Chick-chick-chicken. Come here. Have some of this.'

Chickens are stupid birds, and very greedy. They think everything is food. This one thought the spoon was full of corn. It hopped over. It put its head on one side and looked at the spoon. 'Come on, chicken,' George said. 'Good chicken. Chick-chick-chick.'

The brown hen stretched out its neck towards the spoon and went *peck*. It got a beakful of medicine.

The effect was electric.

'*Oweee!*' shrieked the hen and it shot straight up into the air like a rocket. It went as high as the house.

Then down it came again into the yard, *splosh*. And there it sat with its feathers all sticking straight out from its body. There was a look of amazement on its silly face. George stood watching it. Grandma up on the roof was watching it, too.

The hen got to its feet. It was rather shaky. It was making funny gurgling noises in its throat. Its beak was opening and shutting. It seemed like a pretty sick hen.

'You've done it in, you stupid boy!' Grandma shouted. 'That hen's going to die! Your father'll be after you now! He'll give you socks and serve you right!'

All of a sudden, black smoke started pouring out of the hen's beak.

'It's on fire!' Grandma yelled. 'The hen's on fire!'

George ran to the water-trough to get a bucket of water.

'That hen'll be roasted and ready for eating any moment!' Grandma shouted.

George sloshed the bucket of water over the hen. There was a sizzling sound and the smoke went away.

'Old hen's laid its last egg!' Grandma shouted. 'Hens don't do any laying after they've been on fire!'

Now that the fire was out, the hen seemed better. It stood up properly. It flapped its wings. Then it crouched down low to the ground, as though getting ready to jump. It did jump. It jumped high in the air and turned a complete somersault, then landed back on its feet.

'It's a circus hen!' Grandma shouted from the rooftop. 'It's a flipping acrobat!'

Now the hen

began to

grow.

George had been waiting for this to happen. 'It's growing!' he yelled. 'It's growing, Grandma! Look, it's growing!'

Bigger and bigger . . . taller and taller it grew. Soon the hen was four or five times its normal size.

'Can you see it, Grandma?!' George shouted.

'I can see it, boy!' the old girl shouted back. 'I'm watching it!'

George was hopping about from one foot to the other with excitement, pointing at the enormous hen and shouting, 'It's had the magic medicine, Grandma, and it's growing just like you did!'

But there was a difference between the way the hen was growing and the way Grandma grew. When Grandma grew taller and taller, she got thinner and thinner. The hen didn't. It stayed nice and plump all along. Soon it was taller than George, but it didn't stop there. It went right on growing until it was about as big as a horse. Then it stopped.

'Doesn't it look marvellous, Grandma!' George shouted.

'It's not as tall as me!' Grandma sang out. 'Compared with me, that hen is titchy small! I am the tallest of them all!'

Chapter Nine

The Pig, the Bullocks, the Sheep, the Pony and the Nanny-goat

At that moment, George's mother came back from shopping in the village. She drove her car into the yard and got out. She was carrying a bottle of milk in one hand and a bag of groceries in the other.

The first thing she saw was the gigantic brown hen towering over little George. She dropped the bottle of milk.

Then Grandma started shouting at her from the rooftop, and when she looked up and saw Grandma's head sticking up through the tiles, she dropped the bag of groceries.

'How about that then, eh, Mary?' Grandma shouted. 'I'll bet you've never seen a hen as big as that! That's George's giant hen, that is!'

'But . . . but . . . but . . .' stammered George's mother.

'It's George's magic medicine!' Grandma shouted. 'We've both of us had it, the hen and I!'

'But how in the world did you get up on the roof?' cried the mother.

'I didn't!' cackled the old woman. 'My feet are still standing on the floor in the living-room!'

This was too much for George's mother to understand. She just goggled and gaped. She looked as though she was going to faint.

A second later, George's father appeared. His name was Mr Killy Kranky. Mr Kranky was a small man with bandy legs and a huge head. He was a kind father to George, but he was not an easy person to live with because even the smallest things got him all worked up and excited. The hen standing in the yard was certainly not a small thing, and when Mr Kranky saw it he started jumping about as though something was burning his feet. 'Great heavens!' he cried, waving his arms. 'What's this? What's happened? Where did it come from? It's a giant hen! Who did it?'

'I did,' George said.

'Look at *me*!' Grandma shouted from the rooftop. 'Never mind about the hen! What about *me*?'

Mr Kranky looked up and saw Grandma. 'Shut up, Grandma,' he said. It didn't seem to surprise him that the old girl was sticking up through the roof. It was the hen that excited him. He had never seen anything like it. But then who had?

'It's fantastic!' Mr Kranky shouted, dancing round and round. 'It's colossal! It's gigantic! It's tremendous! It's a miracle! How did you do it, George?'

George started telling his father about the magic medicine. While he was doing this, the big brown hen sat down in the middle of the yard and went *cluck-cluck-cluck . . . cluck-cluck-cluck-cluck-cluck*.

Everyone stared at it.

When it stood up again, there was a brown egg lying there. The egg was the size of a football.

'That egg would make scrambled eggs for twenty people!' Mrs Kranky said.

'George!' Mr Kranky shouted. 'How much of this medicine have you got?'

'Lots,' George said. 'There's a big saucepanful in the kitchen, and this bottle here's nearly full.'

'Come with me!' Mr Kranky yelled, grabbing George by the arm. 'Bring the medicine! For years and years I've been trying to breed bigger and bigger animals. Bigger bulls for beef. Bigger pigs for pork. Bigger sheep for mutton . . .'

They went to the pigsty first.

George gave a spoonful of medicine to the pig.

The pig blew smoke from its nose and jumped about all over the place. Then it grew and grew.

In the end, it looked like this . . .

They went to the herd of fine black bullocks that Mr Kranky was trying to fatten for the market.

George gave each of them some medicine, and this is what happened . . .

Then the sheep . . .

He gave some to his grey pony, Jack Frost . . .

And finally,

just for fun,

he gave some
to Alma,

the nanny-goat . . .

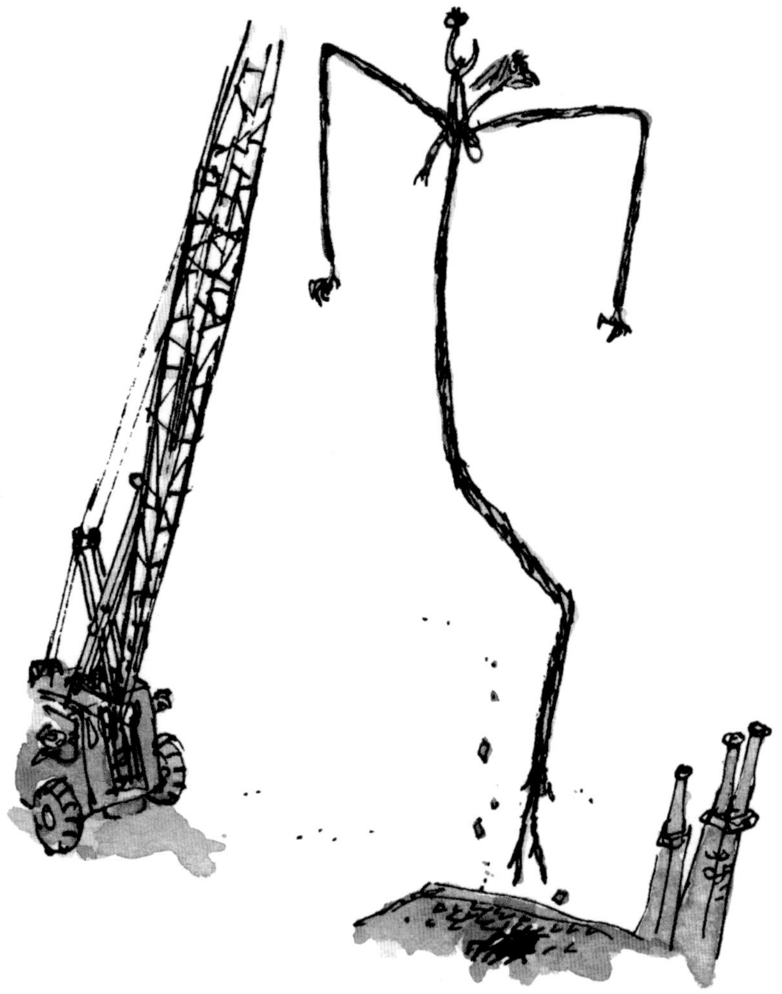

Chapter Ten

A Crane for Grandma

Grandma, from high up on the rooftop, could see everything that was going on and she didn't like what she saw. She wanted to be the centre of attention and nobody was taking the slightest notice of her. George and Mr Kranky were running round and getting excited about the enormous animals. Mrs Kranky was washing up in the kitchen, and Grandma was all alone on the rooftop.

'Hey you!' she yelled. 'George! Get me a cup of tea this minute, you idle little beast!'

'Don't listen to the old goat,' Mr Kranky said. 'She's stuck where she is and a good thing, too.'

'But we can't leave her up there, Dad,' George said. 'What if it rains?'

'George!' Grandma yelled. 'Oh, you horrible little boy! You disgusting little worm! Fetch me a cup of tea at once and a slice of currant cake!'

'We'll have to get her out, Dad,' George said. 'She won't give us any peace if we don't.'

Mrs Kranky came outside and she agreed with George. 'She's my own mother,' she said.

'She's a pain in the neck,' Mr Kranky said.

'I don't care,' Mrs Kranky said. 'I'm not leaving my own mother sticking up through the roof for the rest of her life.'

So in the end, Mr Kranky telephoned the Crane Company and asked them to send their biggest crane out to the house at once.

The crane arrived one hour later. It was on wheels and there were two men inside it. The crane men climbed up on to the roof and put ropes under Grandma's arms. Then she was lifted right up through the roof . . .

In a way, the medicine had done Grandma good. It had not made her any less grumpy or bad-tempered, but it seemed to have cured all her aches and pains, and she was suddenly as frisky as a ferret. As soon as the crane had lowered her to the ground, she ran over to George's huge pony, Jack Frost, and jumped on to his back. This ancient old hag, who was now as tall as a house, then galloped about the farm on the gigantic pony, jumping over trees and sheds and shouting,

'Out of my way! Clear the decks! Stand back, all you miserable midgets or I'll trample you to death!' and other silly things like that.

But because Grandma was now much too tall to get back into the house, she had to sleep that night in the hay-barn with the mice and the rats.

Chapter Eleven

Mr Kranky's Great Idea

The next day, George's father came down to breakfast in a state of greater excitement than ever. 'I've been awake all night thinking about it!' he cried.

'About what, Dad?' George asked him.

'About your marvellous medicine, of course! We can't stop now, my boy! We must start making more of it at once! More and more and more!'

The giant saucepan had been completely emptied the day before because there had been so many sheep and pigs and cows and bullocks to be dosed.

'But why do we need more, Dad?' George asked. 'We've done all our own animals and we've made Grandma feel as frisky as a ferret even though she does have to sleep in the barn.'

'My dear boy,' cried Mr Killy Kranky, 'we need barrels and

barrels of it! Tons and tons! Then we will sell it to every farmer in the world so that all of them can have giant animals! We will build a Marvellous Medicine Factory and sell the stuff in bottles at five pounds a time. We will become rich and you will become famous!'

'But wait a minute, Dad,' George said.

'There's no waiting!' cried Mr Kranky, working himself up so much that he put butter in his coffee and milk on his toast. 'Don't you understand what this tremendous invention of yours is going to do to the world! Nobody will ever go hungry again!'

'Why won't they?' asked George.

'Because one giant cow will give fifty buckets of milk a day!' cried Mr Kranky, waving his arms. 'One giant chicken will make a hundred fried chicken dinners, and one giant pig will give you a thousand pork chops! It's tremendous, my dear boy! It's fantastic! It'll change the world.'

'But wait a minute, Dad,' George said again.

'Don't keep saying wait a minute!' shouted Mr Kranky. 'There isn't a minute to *wait*! We must get cracking at once!'

'Do calm down, my dear,' Mrs Kranky said from the other end of the table. 'And stop putting marmalade on your cornflakes.'

'The heck with my cornflakes!' cried Mr Kranky, leaping up from his chair. 'Come on, George! Let's get going! And the first thing we'll do is to make one more saucepanful as a tester.'

'But Dad,' said little George. 'The trouble is . . .'

'There won't be any trouble, my boy!' cried Mr Kranky. 'How can there possibly be any trouble? All you've got to do is put the same stuff into the saucepan as you did yesterday. And while you're doing it, I'll write down each and every item.

That's how we'll get the magic recipe!'

'But Dad,' George said. 'Please listen to me.'

'Why don't you listen to him?' Mrs Kranky said. 'The boy's trying to tell you something.'

But Mr Kranky was too excited to listen to anyone except himself. 'And then,' he cried, 'when the new mixture is ready, we'll test it out on an old hen just to make absolutely sure we've got it right, and after that we'll all shout hooray and build the giant factory!'

'But Dad . . .'

'Come on then, what is it you want to say?'

'I can't possibly remember all the hundreds of things I put into the saucepan to make the medicine,' George said.

'Of course you can, my dear boy,' cried Mr Kranky. 'I'll help you! I'll jog your memory! You'll get it in the end, you see if you don't! Now then, what was the very first thing you put in?'

'I went up to the bathroom first,' George said. 'I used a lot of things in the bathroom and on Mummy's dressing-table.'

'Come on, then!' cried Mr Killy Kranky. 'Up we go to the bathroom!'

When they got there, they found, of course, a whole lot of empty tubes and empty aerosols and empty bottles. 'That's great,' said Mr Kranky. 'That tells us exactly what you used. If anything is empty, it means you used it.'

So Mr Kranky started making a list of everything that was empty in the bathroom. Then they went to Mrs Kranky's dressing-table. 'A box of powder,' said Mr Kranky, writing it down. 'Helga's hairset. Flowers of Turnips perfume. Terrific. This is going to be easy. Where did you go next?'

'To the laundry-room,' George said. 'But are you sure you haven't missed anything out up here, Dad?'

'That's up to you, my boy,' Mr Kranky said. 'Have I?'

'I don't think so,' George said. So down they went to the laundry-room and once again Mr Kranky wrote down the names of all the empty bottles and cans. 'My goodness me, what a mass of stuff you used!' he cried. 'No wonder it did magic things! Is that the lot?'

'No, Dad, it's not,' George said, and he led his father out to the shed where the animal medicines were kept and showed him the five big empty bottles up on the shelf. Mr Kranky wrote down all their names.

'Anything else?' Mr Kranky asked.

Little George scratched his head and thought and thought but he couldn't remember having put anything else in.

Mr Killy Kranky leapt into his car and drove down to the village and bought new bottles and tubes and cans of everything on his list. He then went to the vet and got a fresh supply of all the animal medicines George had used.

'Now show me how you did it, George,' he said. 'Come along. Show me exactly how you mixed them all together.'

Chapter Twelve

Marvellous Medicine Number Two

They were in the kitchen now and the big saucepan was on the stove. All the things Mr Kranky had bought were lined up near the sink.

'Come along, my boy!' cried Mr Killy Kranky. 'Which one did you put in first?'

'This one,' George said. 'Golden Gloss Hair Shampoo.' He emptied the bottle into the pan.

'Now the toothpaste,' George went on . . . 'And the shaving soap . . . and the face cream . . . and the nail varnish . . .'

'Keep at it, my boy!' cried Mr Kranky, dancing round the kitchen. 'Keep putting them in! Don't stop! Don't pause! Don't hesitate! It's a pleasure, my dear fellow, to watch you work!'

One by one, George poured and squeezed the things into the saucepan. With everything so close at hand, the whole job didn't take him more than ten minutes. But when it was all done, the saucepan didn't somehow seem to be quite as full as it had been the first time.

'*Now* what did you do?' cried Mr Kranky. 'Did you stir it?'

'I boiled it,' George said. 'But not for long. And I stirred it as well.'

So Mr Kranky lit the gas under the saucepan and George stirred the mixture with the same long wooden spoon he had used before. 'It's not brown enough,' George said. 'Wait a minute! I know what I've forgotten!'

'What?' cried Mr Kranky. 'Tell me, quick! Because if we've forgotten even one tiny thing, then it won't work! At least not in the same way.'

'A quart of brown gloss paint,' George said. 'That's what I've forgotten.'

Mr Killy Kranky shot out of the house and into his car like a rocket. He sped down to the village and bought the paint and rushed back again. He opened the can in the kitchen and handed it to George. George poured the paint into the saucepan.

'Ah-ha, that's better,' George said. 'That's more like the right colour.'

'It's boiling!' cried Mr Kranky. 'It's boiling and bubbling, George! Is it ready yet?'

'It's ready,' George said. 'At least I hope it is.'

'Right!' shouted Mr Kranky, hopping about. 'Let's test it! Let's give some to a chicken!'

'My heavens alive, why don't you calm down a bit?' Mrs Kranky said, coming into the kitchen.

'*Calm down?*' cried Mr Kranky. 'You expect me to *calm down* and here we are mixing up the greatest medicine ever discovered in the history of the world! Come along, George! Dip a cupful out of the saucepan and get a spoon and we'll give some to a chicken just to make absolutely certain we've got the correct mixture.'

Outside in the yard, there were several chickens that hadn't had any of George's Marvellous Medicine Number One. They were pecking about in the dirt in that silly way chickens do.

George crouched down, holding out a spoonful of Marvellous Medicine Number Two.

'Come on, chicken,' he said.

'Good chicken. Chick-chick-chick.'

A white chicken with black specks on its feathers looked up at George. It walked over to the spoon and went *peck*.

The effect that Medicine Number Two had on this chicken was not quite the same as the effect produced by Medicine Number One, but it was very interesting. '*Whoooosh!*' shrieked the chicken and it shot six feet up in the air and came down again. Then *sparks* came flying out of its beak, bright yellow sparks of fire, as though someone was sharpening a knife on a grindstone inside its tummy. Then its legs began to grow longer. Its body stayed the same size but the two thin yellow legs got longer and longer and longer . . . and longer still . . .

'What's happening to it?' cried Mr Killy Kranky.

'Something's wrong,' George said.

The legs went on growing and the more they grew, the higher up into the air went the chicken's body. When the legs were about fifteen feet long, they stopped growing. The chicken looked perfectly absurd with its long long legs and its ordinary little body perched high up on top. It was like a chicken on stilts.

'Oh my sainted aunts!' cried Mr Killy Kranky. 'We've got it wrong! This chicken's no good to anybody! It's all legs! No one wants chickens' legs!'

'I must have left something out,' George said.

'I *know* you left something out!' cried Mr Kranky. 'Think, boy, think! What was it you left out?'

'I've got it!' said George.

'What was it, quick?'

'Flea powder for dogs,' George said.

'You mean you put *flea* powder in the first one?'

'Yes, Dad, I did. A whole carton of it.'

'Then that's the answer!'

'Wait a minute,' said George. 'Did we have brown shoe-polish on our list?'

'We did not,' said Mr Kranky.

'I used that, too,' said George.

'Well, no *wonder* it went wrong,' said Mr Kranky. He was already running to his car, and soon he was heading down to the village to buy more flea powder and more shoe-polish.

Chapter Thirteen

Marvellous Medicine Number Three

'Here it is!' cried Mr Killy Kranky, rushing into the kitchen. 'One carton of flea powder for dogs and one tin of brown shoe-polish!'

George poured the flea powder into the giant saucepan. Then he scooped the shoe-polish out of its tin and added that as well.

'Stir it up, George!' shouted Mr Kranky. 'Give it another boil! We've got it this time! I'll bet we've got it!'

After Marvellous Medicine Number Three had been boiled and stirred, George took a cupful of it out into the yard to try it on another chicken. Mr Kranky ran after him, flapping his arms and hopping with excitement. 'Come and watch this one!' he called out to Mrs Kranky. 'Come and watch us turning an ordinary chicken into a lovely great big one that lays eggs as large as footballs!'

'I hope you do better than last time,' said Mrs Kranky, following them out.

'Come on, chicken,' said George, holding out a spoonful of Medicine Number Three. 'Good chicken. Chick-chick-chick-chick-chick. Have some of this lovely medicine.'

A magnificent black cockerel with a scarlet comb came stepping over. The cockerel looked at the spoon and it went *peck*.

'*Cock-a-doodle-do!*' squawked the cockerel, shooting up into the air and coming down again.

'Watch him now!' cried Mr Kranky. 'Watch him grow! Any moment he's going to start getting bigger and bigger!'

Mr Killy Kranky, Mrs Kranky and little George stood in the yard staring at the black cockerel. The cockerel stood quite still. It looked as though it had a headache.

'What's happening to its neck?' Mrs Kranky said.

'It's getting longer,' George said.

'I'll say it's getting longer,' Mrs Kranky said.

Mr Kranky, for once, said nothing.

'Last time it was the legs,' Mrs Kranky said. 'Now it's the neck. Who wants a chicken with a long neck? You can't eat a chicken's neck.'

It was an extraordinary sight. The cockerel's body hadn't grown at all. But the neck was now about six feet long.

'All right, George,' Mr Kranky said. 'What else have you forgotten?'

'I don't know,' George said.

'Oh yes you do,' Mr Kranky said. 'Come along, boy, *think*. There's probably just one vital thing missing and you've got to remember it.'

'I put in some engine oil from the garage,' George said. 'Did you have that on your list?'

'Eureka!' cried Mr Kranky. 'That's the answer! How much did you put in?'

'Half a pint,' George said.

Mr Kranky ran to the garage and found another half-pint of oil. 'And some anti-freeze,' George called after him. 'I sloshed in a bit of anti-freeze.'

Chapter Fourteen

Marvellous Medicine Number Four

Back in the kitchen once again, George, with Mr Kranky watching him anxiously, tipped half a pint of engine oil and some anti-freeze into the giant saucepan.

'Boil it up again!' cried Mr Kranky. 'Boil it and stir it!'

George boiled it and stirred it.

'You'll never get it right,' said Mrs Kranky. 'Don't forget you don't just have to have the same things but you've got to have exactly the same *amounts* of those things. And how can you possibly do that?'

'You keep out of this!' cried Mr Kranky. 'We're doing fine! We've got it this time, you see if we haven't!'

This was George's Marvellous Medicine Number Four, and when it had boiled for a couple of minutes, George once again carried a cupful of it out into the yard. Mr Kranky ran after him. Mrs Kranky followed more slowly. 'You're going to have some mighty queer chickens around here if you go on like this,' she said.

'Dish it out, George!' cried Mr Kranky. 'Give a spoonful to that one over there!' He pointed to a brown hen.

George knelt down and held out the spoon with the new medicine in it. 'Chick-chick,' he said. 'Try some of this.'

The brown hen walked over and looked at the spoon. Then it went *peck*.

'*Owch!*' it said. Then a funny whistling noise came out of its beak.

'Watch it grow!' shouted Mr Kranky.

'Don't be too sure,' said Mrs Kranky. 'Why is it whistling like that?'

'Keep quiet, woman!' cried Mr Kranky. 'Give it a chance!'

They stood there staring at the brown hen.

'It's getting smaller,' George said. 'Look at it, Dad. It's shrinking.'

And indeed it was. In less than a minute, the hen had shrunk so much it was no bigger than a new-hatched chick. It looked ridiculous.

Chapter Fifteen

Goodbye Grandma

'There's still something you've left out,' Mr Kranky said.

'I can't think what it could be,' George said.

'Give it up,' Mrs Kranky said. 'Pack it in. You'll never get it right.'

Mr Kranky looked very forlorn.

George looked pretty fed up, too. He was still kneeling on the ground with the spoon in one hand and the cup full of medicine in the other. The ridiculous tiny brown hen was walking slowly away.

At that point, Grandma came striding into the yard. From her enormous height, she glared down at the three people below her and she shouted, 'What's going on around here? Why hasn't anyone brought me my morning cup of tea? It's bad enough having to sleep in the yard with the rats and mice but I'll be blowed if I'm going to starve as well! No tea! No eggs and bacon! No buttered toast!'

'I'm sorry, Mother,' Mrs Kranky said. 'We've been terribly busy. I'll get you something right away.'

'Let George get it, the lazy little brute!' Grandma shouted.

Just then, the old woman spotted the cup in George's hand. She bent down and peered into it. She saw that it was full of brown liquid. It looked very much like tea. 'Ho-ho!' she cried. 'Ha-ha! So that's your little game, is it! You look after yourself all right, don't you! You make quite sure *you've* got a nice cup of morning tea! But you didn't think to bring one to your poor old Grandma! I always knew you were a selfish pig!'

'No, Grandma,' George said. 'This isn't . . .'

'Don't lie to me, boy!' the enormous old hag shouted. 'Pass it up here this minute!'

'No!' cried Mrs Kranky. 'No, Mother, don't! That's not for you!'

'Now *you're* against me, too!' shouted Grandma. 'My own daughter trying to stop me having my breakfast! Trying to starve me out!'

Mr Kranky looked up at the horrid old woman and he smiled sweetly. 'Of course it's for you, Grandma,' he said. 'You take it and drink it while it's nice and hot.'

'Don't think I won't,' Grandma said, bending down from her great height and reaching out a huge horny hand for the cup. 'Hand it over, George.'

'No, no, Grandma!' George cried out, pulling the cup away. 'You mustn't! You're not to have it!'

'Give it to me, boy!' yelled Grandma.

'Don't!' cried Mrs Kranky. 'That's George's Marvellous . . .'

'Everything's George's round here!' shouted Grandma. 'George's this, George's that! I'm fed up with it!' She snatched the cup out of little George's hand and carried it high up out of reach.

'Drink it up, Grandma,' Mr Kranky said, grinning hugely. 'Lovely tea.'

'No!' the other two cried. 'No, no, no!'

But it was too late. The ancient beanpole had already put the cup to her lips, and in one gulp she swallowed everything that was in it.

'Mother!' wailed Mrs Kranky. 'You've just drunk fifty doses of George's Marvellous Medicine Number Four and look what one tiny spoonful did to that little old brown hen!'

But Grandma didn't even hear her. Great clouds of steam were already pouring out of her mouth and she was beginning to whistle.

'This is going to be interesting,' Mr Kranky said, still grinning.

'Now you've done it!' cried Mrs Kranky, glaring at her husband. 'You've cooked the old girl's goose!'

'I didn't do anything,' Mr Kranky said.

'Oh, yes you did! You told her to drink it!'

A tremendous hissing sound was coming from above their heads. Steam was shooting out of Grandma's mouth and nose and ears and whistling as it came.

'She'll feel better after she's let off a bit of steam,' Mr Kranky said.

'She's going to blow up!' Mrs Kranky wailed. 'Her boiler's going to burst!'

'Stand clear,' Mr Kranky said.

George was quite alarmed. He stood up and ran back a few paces. The jets of white steam kept squirting out of the skinny old hag's head, and the whistling was so high and shrill it hurt the ears.

'Call the fire brigade!' cried Mrs Kranky. 'Call the police! Man the hose-pipes!'

'Too late,' said Mr Kranky, looking pleased.

'Grandma!' shrieked Mrs Kranky. 'Mother! Run to the drinking-trough and put your head under the water!'

But even as she spoke, the whistling suddenly stopped and the steam disappeared. That was when Grandma began to get smaller. She had started off with her head as high as the roof of the house, but now she was coming down fast.

'Watch this, George!' Mr Kranky shouted, hopping around the yard and flapping his arms. 'Watch what happens when someone's had fifty spoonfuls instead of one!'

Very soon, Grandma was back to normal height.

'Stop!' cried Mrs Kranky. 'That's just right.'

But she didn't stop. Smaller and smaller she got . . . down and down she went. In another half minute she was no bigger than a bottle of lemonade.

'How d'you feel, Mother?' asked Mrs Kranky anxiously. Grandma's tiny face still bore the same foul and furious expression it had always had. Her eyes, no bigger now than little keyholes, were blazing with anger. 'How do I *feel*?' she yelled. 'How d'you *think* I feel? How would *you* feel if you'd been a glorious giant a minute ago and suddenly you're a miserable midget?'

'She's still going!' shouted Mr Kranky gleefully. 'She's still getting smaller!'

And by golly, she was.

When she was no bigger than a cigarette, Mrs Kranky made a grab for her. She held her in her hands and she cried, 'How do I stop her getting smaller still?'

'You can't,' said Mr Kranky. 'She's had fifty times the right amount.'

'I *must* stop her!' Mrs Kranky wailed. 'I can hardly see her as it is!'

'Catch hold of each end and pull,' Mr Kranky said.

By then, Grandma was the size of a match-stick and still shrinking fast.

A moment later, she was no bigger than a pin . . .

Then a pumpkin seed . . .

Then . . .

Then . . .

'Where is she?' cried Mrs Kranky. 'I've lost her!'

'Hooray,' said Mr Kranky.

'She's gone! She's disappeared completely!' cried Mrs Kranky.

'That's what happens to you if you're grumpy and bad-tempered,' said Mr Kranky. 'Great medicine of yours, George.'

George didn't know what to think.

For a few minutes, Mrs Kranky kept wandering round with a puzzled look on her face, saying, 'Mother, where are you? Where've you gone? Where've you got to? How can I find you?' But she calmed down quite quickly. And by lunchtime, she was saying, 'Ah well, I suppose it's all for the best, really. She was a bit of a nuisance around the house, wasn't she?'

'Yes,' Mr Kranky said. 'She most certainly was.'

George didn't say a word. He felt quite trembly. He knew something tremendous had taken place that morning. For a few brief moments he had touched with the very tips of his fingers the edge of a magic world.

There's more to Roald Dahl than great stories . . .

Did you know that 10% of author royalties* from this book go to help the work of the Roald Dahl charities?

Roald Dahl's Marvellous Children's Charity aims to raise as much money as possible to make seriously ill children's lives better because it believes that every child has the right to a marvellous life.

This marvellous charity helps thousands of children each year in the UK living with serious conditions of the blood and the brain – causes important to Roald Dahl in his lifetime.

Whether by providing nurses, equipment, carers or toys, the charity helps to care for children with conditions including acquired brain injury, epilepsy and blood disorders such as sickle cell disease.

Can you do something marvellous to help others?
Find out how at **www.roalddahlcharity.org**

The Roald Dahl Museum and Story Centre, based in Great Missenden just outside London, is in the Buckinghamshire village where Roald Dahl lived and wrote. At the heart of the Museum, intended to inspire a love of reading and writing, is his unique archive of letters and manuscripts. As well as two fun-packed biographical galleries, the Museum boasts an interactive Story Centre and is now the home of his famous writing hut. It is a place for the family and teachers and their pupils to explore the exciting world of creativity and literacy.

www.roalddahlmuseum.org

Roald Dahl's Marvellous Children's Charity (RDMCC) is a registered charity no. 1004230.
The Roald Dahl Museum and Story Centre (RDMSC) is a registered charity no. 1085853.
The Roald Dahl Charitable Trust is a registered charity no. 1119330
and supports the work of RDMCC and RDMSC.

*Donated royalties are net of commission.